A BAND OF BROTHERS

A BAND OF BROTHERS

STORIES FROM VIETNAM

WALTER McDONALD

TEXAS TECH UNIVERSITY PRESS, LUBBOCK, TEXAS
1989

A Band of Brothers is a cycle of short stories. The characters and events in these stories are fictional. Any similarity to persons living or dead is purely coincidental.

Printed in the United States of America

This book was set in ITC New Baskerville and printed on acid-free paper that meets the guidelines for permanence and durability of the Committee on Production Guidelines for Book Longevity of the Council on Library Resources.♾

Design by Cameron Poulter

Grateful acknowledgment is made to editors who published the following stories, some with different titles in earlier versions: "Bien Dien," *The Sam Houston Literary Review*; "Croom," *Crosscurrents*; "Lebowitz," *Re: Artes Liberales*; "Mayday," *The Village Advocate*; "New Guy," *New and Experimental Literature*; "Rockets," *New Mexico Humanities Review*; "The Send-off," *The Bicentennial Collection of Texas Short Stories*; "Snow Job," *Quartet*; "The Track," *Sam Houston Literary Review, Northwest, The Village Advocate, Vietnam Voices: Perspectives on the War Years, 1941–1982,* and *Prize Stories: Texas Institute of Letters*; "Turning On," *Vision*; "Waiting for the End," *Descant*; "Why Randy Wayne Crashed and Burned," *Texas Stories and Poems* and *Clarity: A Text on Writing*.

William Faulkner, *The Wishing Tree*. Copyright © 1964. Reprinted by permission of Random House, Inc.

Library of Congress Cataloging-in-Publication Data
McDonald, Walter.
    A band of brothers : stories from Vietnam / Walter McDonald.
        p. cm.
    ISBN 0-89672-208-2. — ISBN 0-89672-209-0 (pbk.)
    1. Vietnamese Conflict,—1961–1975—Fiction. I. Title.
PS3563.A2914B36   1989
813'.54—dc20   89-36088
                                                                                CIP

Texas Tech University Press
Lubbock, Texas 79409-1037 USA

For Jesse, John, Joe, Dave,
and Kelly

"Rather proclaim it, Westmoreland, . . .
That he which hath no stomach to this fight,
Let him depart . . .
He that outlives this day . . . and see[s] old age . . .
Will stand a tip-toe when this day is named . . .
Then will he strip his sleeve and show his scars,
And say 'These wounds I had on Crispin's day.' . . .
We few, we happy few, we band of brothers;
For he to-day that sheds his blood with me
Shall be my brother."

—Shakespeare, *Henry the Fifth*, IV, iii

"I was in a war," the little old man said to Alice's husband.
"Which one?" Alice's husband asked.
"I never did know," the little old man answered. "There
was a lot of folks in it, I remember."
. . . .
"Who won the war you were in?" Dulcie asked.
"I don't know, ma'am," the little old man answered. "I
didn't."

—William Faulkner, *The Wishing Tree*.

CONTENTS

FOREWORD

War has always been hard to understand. Why here? Why now? Why in this way? Why me? And, above all, why in the name of God and humanity can't we seem to live without it?

War has also been hard to explain. Writing about war to someone who has never been in war is like explaining marriage to a eunuch. It's a different world. It's a doubly different world because military life is already difficult enough to explain, and wartime military life is distinctly different from peacetime military life.

It's particularly difficult explaining war to Americans because most Americans know little of war. No living and native-born American has seen bombs falling on his neighborhood, enemy troops marching down his street, or tanks rolling across his lawn. Most American citizens do not know what war looks like or feels like or smells like. It is doubly difficult to explain war to Americans because, unfortunately, they think they do know.

They think they know what war is like because they live in the age of information and they have the facts. They have seen war as it has been represented by artists. They have seen paintings of the sweep and grandeur of battle, with flags waving and generals prancing on white horses. But the lines are too clean, the colors too bright, and no matter how accurate, paintings convey none of the stench, the incredible carnage, the shrieks and moans of the frightened, the wounded, and the dying.

They have read poems glorifying heroes and heard the songs of the victors. Poetry, trapped in its very form, lends refinement to horror, as in Dylan Thomas's "A Refusal to

Mourn the Death, by fire, of a Child in London," or a pattern of pleasure to meaningless pain, as in Randall Jarrell's "Death of the Ball Turret Gunner." Rhythmical, rational, systematic, poetry cannot capture the sprawling chaos of war.

Fiction writers, at least those who are after understanding rather than spoils, are caught in drama, narrative drive, and the other elements of a good story, the form more important than the function. They must challenge the appealing heroics of Homer and Shakespeare and describe the grotesque and obscene without driving away the sickened reader. Unlike poetry, fiction must appeal to masses who have not been trained to recognize truth, much less applaud it.

Some citizens, perhaps, have heard the scabrous stories of warriors whose tongues are unfamiliar with heroics, and virtue, and the righteousness of their cause, but such stories seem pointless, and the warriors retire into obscurity, their medals tarnished with the memory of what they have seen and done.

Generals write books filled with grandiose schemes, fantastic strategies, and glorious and meaningful triumphs.

Journalism offers limited ways of seeing selected pictures, and most easily follows the path of counting the dead, weighing the bombs, and measuring progress and loss in dollars and in feet.

History, eventually, attempts to put the puzzle together in a rational scheme, for those who read history, and to answer the who and how and where and when, but never the why.

The movies combined the sweep and grandeur of painting with the heroics and songs of the poets, and became the propaganda arm of the government to give us good and evil based on the color of one's uniform. Everyone in American, English or Russian uniform was good. Everyone in German or Japanese uniform was bad, and the death of each of them made the world a better place in which to live. Italians were bad too, but you could feel sorry for them if you also felt contempt.

However, the movies did not explain that many war criminals wore no uniform at all. Or that many of those on both sides who did wear uniforms were unwilling warriors, caught up by force of law, or patriotism, or some personal need for escape from present misery or private misgiving. The movies did not explain evil men who looked like ourselves. But the movies gave us real made-in-Hollywood carnage, real safe-in-Hollywood courage, real money-in-the bank patriotism.

It was not just that the actors pretended hunger, or fear, or courage, but that they pretended to know, pretended to have experienced, and, therefore, pretended authority for telling others what war was like. Houses were burned in war, whole cities of them; children were killed, whole schools of them. But not by Americans. Only the implacably evil Germans and Japanese killed civilians on the screen.

Poets and painters gave us war as a terrible beauty. Fiction writers gave us war as a palatable tale of drama and import. Journalism gave us war as facts, lists, places, men and matériel. Warriors gave us war as pointless anecdote. Generals gave us war as the moral equivalent of free enterprise. History gave us war as compressed biography.

The movies gave us innocence. The painters, poets, journalists, generals, and historians had said otherwise. They had pointed at an America that knew wars for economic advantage and political gain, that knew slavery and, after slavery, sweat shops, child labor, and the importation of immigrants to maintain the semblance of slavery, an America that knew Antietam, Dresden, and Hiroshima. But the movies gave us real made-in-Hollywood innocence. And we basked in that innocence. And we believed we knew.

Then came Vietnam. Then came television into our living rooms. Television gave us death in living color, with the screen a stage for the most outrageous and attention-getting sound bite. We saw professional soldiers playing the beast and the clown to grab ten seconds of the nation's attention that was focused on the screen. We saw men in American uniforms who looked the way the enemy was supposed to have looked, men who didn't die on glorious fields of battle but in mud, in filth, in unhallowed ground their comfortable compatriots would not walk on. Men who were not John-Wayne-tough, or Ronald-Reagan-slick. Men who did not glory in the job their country had given them of killing other men, or delight when the job was well done.

It wasn't My Lai that showed us the face behind our innocent mask; it was Washington, and Wall Street, and that eye in the living room. War wasn't like this in the movies. War had never been presented like this by those who heroically and patriotically stayed behind to help civilian morale and pick up loose change. And the shock went deep. What had happened to innocence? What had happened to our children? What had happened to America?

War is difficult to understand. That's why we link killing for political and economic causes with quasi-religious slogans, like killing some men to free others, or destroying nations to make the world safe for democracy, or waging war to end war. And in the best wars, the good wars, the holy wars, the linkage holds, at least for true believers.

The war in Vietnam is the latest war we can't understand, and it is one of the most difficult to understand because the shock went deep. We thought we knew; we had seen it in the movies. We can't understand, because John F. Kennedy's linkage—to bear any burden, meet any hardship, support any friend, oppose any enemy in the name of liberty—was applauded as poetry but not as practice. And because no one ever defined what was at stake, or what our intent was, or what would constitute victory.

We can't, and don't, understand because we can't accept that war was always like this. We would have to give up our dream of good wars, of righteous killing, have to give up Ivanhoe, and Scarlett O'Hara's brave idealistic and tragic

Ashley, and John Wayne and his affably innocent sidekick, Ronald Reagan. We'd have to give up heroic warriors who never suffered doubt or diarrhea, who killed without remorse and triumphed without guilt. And with only a backward glance at their fallen comrades and enemies. "Sorry about that, pilgrim."

The painters and poets, warriors and generals, journalists and historians, movie and television producers have rushed in, some to trivialize what were life and death matters to others, some to help us to understanding. Walter McDonald is one of the latter, first with poetry and now with short stories.

McDonald is many things: pilot, professor, poet, and writer of short stories. Yet, above all these things, or in all these things, he is a teacher. Not an educator—that word is too puffed with self-importance—or pedagogue, but a teacher in its simplest and finest meaning; a person who lives what he means. A teacher like Jesus of Nazareth or St. Francis of Assisi.

The measure of McDonald as writer and teacher is taken in *A Band of Brothers* because he brings to the subject of Vietnam the experience of a pilot who went to Vietnam and the sensitivity and economy of a poet. There is drama here, but not enough for commercial publishers. There is narrative drive, but not enough for speed readers. *A Band of Brothers* is not sensational or violent enough to capture headlines, but it is true enough to capture heads and hearts.

Others have given us the attentuated language, the military jargon, the grotesquery of combat, the madness that accompanies war and is mirrored in its attendants. And those elements are found here, but McDonald doesn't give us good guys and bad guys. He gives us human beings trying to remain humane despite inhuman demands. This is Vietnam. A piece of it. It's not clean. It's not heroic. It's not the war as seen in movies or TV. But it is real in a way they will never be. And it is told in painful detail by a tough and tender storyteller who avoids trivializing death, even the death of the enemy. Who avoids sentimentalizing fear and courage, even the courage of patriots.

This is not a book about hawks or doves, or for hawks or doves, those simplistic body bags with which we try to cover our ignorance. This is a book about human beings in a baffling and dangerous world, and it is for human beings who want to know, and who want to care, without distinctions based on race, creed, or uniform. This is not a book for casual, uncritical, uncaring readers idling away a few minutes between TV commercials about the good life.

Walt McDonald doesn't want that kind of painless, bloodless understanding or acceptance. He doesn't deserve that kind of easy judgment. Neither do the men whose souls are captured here.

Robert Flynn
San Antonio, Texas

NEW GUYS

# NEW GUY

They warned me that VC in peasant pajamas shoot at planes coming in for landing. So I tucked my chin and leaned back from the tiny porthole window. If Colonel Tydings, sitting next to me with his legs crossed, saw me then, he must have thought oh man, one of those. But I didn't want to get pranged before seeing some of the war. I kept telling myself.

The C-130 transport bounced all over the sky on final approach, the engines louder than anything I'd ever heard. The cabin lights dimmed and the whole plane hammered and groaned and I smelled gasoline and thought man, we'll blow up.

I glanced at Colonel Tydings and he swept both hands downward.

"Landing gear!" he yelled calmly.

I nodded and turned to the window so he wouldn't notice how big my eyes felt. Bien Dien Air Base stretched ahead, miles of concrete and Quonset huts and nothing but jungle all beyond. There were supposed to be a river and a refugee village of several thousand and a road, and on the other side of the plane the beaches of the South China Sea. But from my window, all I could see at first glance was like a wilderness development that hadn't worked out.

The landing gear jolted into place and the aircraft nosed down steeply. I couldn't see the runway, but the ramps and buildings began looming closer and closer and the jungle dropped sharply behind and we were over the base. The engines cut, popping and crashing, and the plane leveled out for touchdown. With strange sounds blasting my ears, I expected to see rockets exploding everywhere and the black-pajamaed Vietcong crouching from building to building, tossing satchel charges.

But I saw only a sprawling base that loomed abandoned, with a dozen or so empty F-4s in their sandbagged revetments. I saw no destroyed buildings as I had expected, no signs of life at all.

All the way up from Saigon, Colonel Tydings had briefed me about the massive buildup north of Bien Dien and the rocket attacks on the base and Plei Nhon, the village to the west. "We won't even get in today," he had warned, "if they haven't filled the runway holes yet."

The C-130 held in the air, slower, massive like a thunderstorm about to hit, then slammed onto the runway and I thought for a second we had landed in a rocket crater. The plane shuddered with a sudden lurch as if accelerating to take off again, but the runway slowed and with a whine the flaps began rising flush with the wing and the brakes grabbed and released, grabbed and released. And still going fast as if the pilot were hurrying for cover, the plane swerved off onto a taxiway, the wing tip passing several feet over the camouflaged helmet of a lone air policeman in a sandbagged guardhouse a few yards off the runway. He stared at us, forlorn and isolated, as we hurtled past.

Bien Dien Bay, oddly green and deserted, churned in with whitecaps from the vast South China Sea. The C-130 turned sharply again and rolled toward the flight-line buildings.

"As I said," Colonel Tydings went on as the noise dropped, "I'll be here a couple of days, if you need any help. Nose around all you can. Catch a few flights. Take in all the briefings. See if there's any action going on. I'll tell Colonel Dodd you're to be given free access. And just tell it like it is, Mosely, what you see. It's not how you feel about something that counts, but what really happens."

He paused, inspecting me. "Got your cassette?"

"Yes, sir."

"Tapes?"

I said I did.

"Good. And don't be in any hurry," Colonel Tydings said, and dropped his fist on my shoulder. "There's no deadline for truth."

The big plane wheeled up in front of base operations and plunged to a halt, engines shuddering. A crewman ran to open the door.

"This is it," Colonel Tydings said, coming erect. He took his thin blue briefcase and hurried forward.

I followed, feeling eyes on me. I imagined a sniper waiting to get me the minute I stepped through the door. But I held my flight bag high and jumped, hitting the concrete heavily in my stiff new combat boots. Colonel Tydings was halfway to base ops, so I ran through the prop wash to catch up. No sniper fire. Nothing in real life ever happens at the dramatic moment.

Tydings got a jeep and driver and we rode to the Tactical Operations Center, about a half mile down the flight line. TOC was a low set of barracks jammed together to form an H. There were no trees, no bushes, not even a blade of grass or weed, as if a Ranchhand operation of C-123s had sprayed Agent Orange on the area before the base was built.

On the wall was an eight-foot shield splashed silver and blue with a ghostly pilot in a crash helmet, fondling a long-boned nude with big lips and narrow sleepy eyes. The ghost wore a silk scarf. The nude, faded by many monsoons, looked more like a whore than a centerfold. In Gothic crimson script across the top, the shield read 66th Fighter Wing. Under that the squadrons were listed—the 633rd TFS, 635th TFS, 688th TFS, and 697th TFS—with black lines drawn across all but the 688th. And in black blurred letters under the reclining nude's bottom, Phantoms.

How, I wondered, will I ever make Sheila believe this.

Inside, Colonel Tydings huddled with a civilian and five pilots. Only one—short, fat, and scowling—glanced at me. They stood together facing Tydings like a space posse before a shoot-out. They all wore drab green flight suits, with tight G-suits like chaps sectioned around the waist and thighs and zipped down the inside legs, making them look bowlegged. All wore .38s crisscrossed with bullet loops, all wore gray and green gloves and silver-edged flight caps and silk scarves. The patch of the phantom and the lady, more intriguing in miniature, was on each pilot's shoulder. They all stood cool, with arms crossed like their leader, Colonel Bobby Dodd, who at six-five towered above Tydings.

I recognized him on sight, shoulders bulging, mustache flaring. Colonel Dodd was famous even in the States. A genuine, publicized hero, a MiG-killer, both in Korea and here. An all-American from Michigan who could have played for the Lions, if he weren't born to fly. When he was twenty, already as famous as Blanchard and Davis from West Point, he had married an heiress and could have bought his own airline. But when forces in Vietnam were reduced last year, he passed up an assignment in Florida as commander of a real four-squadron wing and certain promotion to general to stay on until the end, flying as a mere one-squadron wing commander. Just looking at him scowling down at whatever bad news Colonel Tydings had brought from Saigon, I could tell he was loving it.

"It'll keep till after the mission," I heard him booming at Colonel Tydings. His deep voice resonated like a tail pipe.

"But this is urgent," Colonel Tydings said. "Can't one of these go up for you?"

Colonel Dodd raised his massive head with the pilot's disdain for officers without wings. "It's not their turn," he said, his gaze off somewhere in the blue.

Tydings wasn't a new guy like me, though. He must have

taken that from pilots every day of his career. Maybe that's why he learned judo.

"It's from General Pitts," he insisted, his eyes leveled at Dodd's chest.

Colonel Dodd grinned, one side of his mustache arching. "Old Harry? What does that old bastard want?"

"Top Secret," Tydings said quietly, conspiratorially. "Need-to-know basis only."

"Jack," Colonel Dodd chided. "What's to know? The NVA are massing north of here, they've started hitting us every other night, Plei Nhon and Bien Dien villages will soon get pounded to hell." He looked down at Tydings. "If we don't get up there and locate and destroy the build-up soon. So what else is new?"

Colonel Tydings waited, not smiling. Colonel Dodd looked at his watch, a black chronometer on his huge powerful wrist.

"I'll be down at 2100," he said, scowling at the dials.

"All right," Tydings said, his voice patient. "It'll keep till then."

Colonel Dodd turned away but Tydings caught his arm. "Bobby," Tydings said. "Here's a new *SNOW* writer who'll be observing for a few months. Lieutenant Mosely. Says they call him 'Moose.' I hope you'll show him the war."

I felt the others watching me with the same superior disdain as Colonel Dodd.

"Moose?" Colonel Dodd said, his handlebars lifting over something filthy.

"Yes, sir," I said, stepping forward to offer my hand. I didn't know whether to salute or kneel. "Little Moose, actually."

"Little Moose," Colonel Dodd repeated, looking down as if that were somehow better. At last he returned my salute and shook my hand, his glove smelling of tobacco and jet fuel. I saw him watching my wingless tans. "You a boxer?"

"No, sir. Wrestler, Ball State."

"Any good?" he asked, no twinkle in his eyes.

"All-conference," I said. I was also honorable mention all-American one year, but it seemed best not to brag.

He nodded, half-satisfied. "So. You've come to the fracas." He turned his head to the older, slender civilian who had waited without talking. "What do you think, Vince? Will the Moose here get to see any action?"

The civilian, his dry face tight and porous like a bone, grinned up at me. I recognized him from the flight to San Francisco last week, before my port call. He lounged on a black plastic couch like a man who had found a home in Nam. Slouched, he stared back at me with a wry, curiously patient grin as if he knew me from somewhere. Bald on the front, he was a thin man probably much taller than Tydings and me. The skin on his face was stretched like a yellowed lampshade, and he munched snuff behind dark lips creased with deep vertical scars, as if they had been stitched.

"Powell," the man said to me, shaking hands, his hand cold and bony. "Vince Powell. For a minute I thought you were someone I met coming over the other day. Freckled kid," he said to Tydings. "Eddy something. Just out of radar school."

"I remember," I said.

"They put him in the 259th," Powell added, "on Pimah Mountain."

Tydings smiled grimly. "He won't last long."

Powell nodded. "They'll knock out that radar site any day now."

His lips, wrinkled like stitches, swelled over gums crammed full of teeth. He guarded a black bag beside his feet, a little larger than a bowling bag, wrinkled and cracked from long use.

Colonel Tydings said, "Vince was here before the first marines hit the beach in '65. He's head of CISCO, the casualty investigation team. He came down from Da Nang this morning to check the damage. Vince and I go way back together. He taught me everything I know."

Powell grinned, his eyes dry and hollow. Snuff showed at the corners of his mouth, oozing also at the vertical creases all along the lips. He bent beside his legs and opened the bag, slipping his hand in and out for a cup, green and waxy like pure jade. He lifted it to his lips and spat.

Powell smiled, as if measuring my head for size. "Wrestling's no good, here. You need to be a runner. Those little Vietnamese don't have half your muscles, but they can run all day and all night on a handful of rice and marsh water."

Tydings agreed. "Go down to the track, Mosely. You'll find guys any hour of the day jogging their guts out, scared they'll get caught somewhere and have to run for their lives."

Powell spat quietly into the cup and grinned.

Colonel Tydings took my arm and shook it fatherly. "He's just a new guy, Vince. He'll find out he's safer here than on the freeways back home."

The pilots smirked, their crossed arms tightening with glee.

I heard a *thump* in the distance, followed by *thump thump*. No one reacted but two captains, whose eyes met quickly. One of them—they could have been twins—melted away from the room like a shadow.

"Look, Bobby." Tydings lowered his voice, his lips glistening. "You and I know if this whole area doesn't fall before the cease-fire it'll be air power that saves it." He paused to let Colonel Dodd agree, then said, "Whatever happens, I want the whole story recorded. I want the last American on the last flight home to be a *SNOW* writer. The Little Moose here may be my man."

Later, after hours of briefings, Colonel Tydings finally turned me loose to find my way to the barracks. In the distance there were the booms and rumble like thunder, the strange new sounds of war. I could hardly believe they were real. Listening, I climbed the outside stairs in darkness and with a penlight found the room number that matched the key.

The louvered door was covered with screen wire, and the top three feet of the wall were also screened. Like most others in the hootch, this room was dark, but I knocked anyway, then let myself in and found the light switch.

The room was larger than I expected, dim, smudged near the ceiling, and bleak, with four metal beds and chests and several chairs. It had an adjoining lounge, and a jagged scar ran up the wall and across the ceiling and down behind the unmade bed.

Crossing to the bed on the far wall, I passed through strange layers of incense, like dusty burial spices. I dropped my flight bag on the faded gray troop mattress and sat down. The springs sagged, worn out. It had been a long war.

I saw the incense burner, flanking a silver candelabra on one chest. There was a Star of David in one corner of the mirror, and on the chest a coffee pot and china cups and a row of books with thick dark bindings. There were several framed pictures too far away to make out and a silver-quilled pen set and a marble valet tray.

The other chests were bare like mine, and only the beds made with Air Force blue wool blankets promised other occupants. I wondered if they were out flying. I wondered if Sheila was out tonight.

Sheila. Vague memories of long straight hair and peaceful eyes and granny glasses and a body made for bed and protest marches. Cold bitch. The night before leaving for my port call I waded a mile through the snow, piled deep on campus. And then all night in her dorm, the musk-scented candle glowing, the FM throbbing rock, my assignment to Vietnam lay unsheathed between us on the bed like Siegfried's sword.

Sheila, more than half a world away, no longer real. The booms out there in the jungle, they were real, the roar of jet fighters landing and taking off were real, all the sounds of war so familiar on television that they had seemed mere history were now the limits of my life. I wanted my new roommates to hurry back. I wanted tomorrow to come, I wanted to fly the missions Tydings told me to fly and do whatever I had to do and get it over.

I found extra bedding in the closet and made my bed and propped up to read the *SNOW* reports I had brought along from Saigon. I was halfway through the battle of An Loc when I heard them climbing the stairs. Loud, drunk, they stumbled down the hall into another room. Others joined them, and I thought about going over. But I needed to read about the destruction of Quang Tri, the town shelled into rubble last year, the way Colonel Tydings predicted Plei Nhon and Bien Dien villages, a few miles to the west, would soon be attacked. And all of us here on the base.

At midnight, at the page describing the week when Quang Tri was being pounded daily by six thousand shells, mortars, and rockets, I could hardly hear myself think for the racket down the hall.

Someone in another room yelled, "Shut up and let me get some sleep!"

And a voice yelled back, "Get your ass out here and try to make me, Berrigan!"

Drunk, thick with scorn, that voice I was sure was Major Shackler's, one of Colonel Dodd's staff officers. He broke defiantly into a song about navigators and queers in hell, and others joined in at the tops of their lungs. A bottle smashed on the ground down below.

I marked the report and turned out the light, feeling my way back to the bed, all but asleep in spite of the party and the heavy explosions thudding a distant cadence to their singing. Light from down the hall filtered through the screen and my eyes adjusted to the dark as sleep loomed over me like a bad dream.

I fell tumbling out of bed, yelling "Good God!" before I hit the floor. The sharp, earsplitting blast, rocket or bomb, was gone by then, but I could hear it spasm on and on in my brain.

I lay shaking in terror on the floor, certain I'd be dead in a second when the next one hit. Suddenly, bursting like a hailstorm, the fallout battered down on the room. I grabbed for the bed springs and pulled under, scraping my head on the low rail.

Silence. I expected a siren and gunfire and the scream of Phantoms taking off, but there was nothing. I lay there wedged under the bed, afraid the next rocket would be a direct hit. I didn't know. I thought of a bomb set off by Vietcong sappers, and I heard someone running on the stairs.

I slid out from under the bed and crouched my way toward the door. Then I saw movement near the chest with the candlesticks and heard a zipping sound. I tensed, ready to spring.

"Hi," the other said, zipping his flight suit.

"Hey," I said, and straightened up in my underwear, feeling new and very grateful.

"You're the Little Moose," the voice said rapidly. "I'm Lebowitz. I flew tonight, and you were asleep when I came in."

Winding slowly, a siren a block away screamed louder and higher and reached a shriek, falling and rising in wavering panic.

I watched the dim movements of Lebowitz sitting on the bed and tugging his boots on.

"That your first rocket?" he asked. He had a thin high-keyed voice that didn't fit his apparent calm.

"Right," I said, trying to sound cool. "Scares hell out of you, doesn't it?"

Lebowitz snapped on a lamp, his thin face drawn, almost emaciated, his eyes deepset in dark hollow sockets, his stiff hair pepper white.

"You can always tell a rocket," he said, strapping a watch to his wrist. "There's a certain rich deep *crack*! about it, like a loud thunderclap and a wooden screen door slamming hard all at once. Richer than a mortar."

Scared as I was, I felt foolish standing there in my shorts, the siren wailing outside. "What do we do now?" I asked.

"Grab your pants and let's get to the bunker."

I did as he said, wondering if it was wise to go downstairs and across the yard to the bunker. At Tan Son Nhut the disaster control officer had briefed the half-dozen new guys on what a rocket can do to a man. Lie flat, he had said. The worst thing you could do after an attack starts is to run for cover. You might survive a rocket burst ten yards away if you're flat on your face, he said, but if you're on your knees it'll mangle you like hamburger.

Lebowitz paused and looked at the third bed, the white sheet dangling. "You coming, Hooker?"

I was stunned to see legs under the bed, a body huddled on the floor and against the wall. I couldn't see the man's face, but I recognized the fear hunching him rigidly in the shadow of his bed.

"Come on," Lebowitz said to me.

Pulling on my tans, I asked, "Where's our other roommate?"

"Croom?" He scooped change from the chest and dropped it in a pocket. "Out walking around. He's an insomniac."

"When does he sleep?"

"Doesn't. Relaxes at night by walking the base perimeter."

Lebowitz opened the door and I fell in with him, zipping my pants as I ran.

"Isn't that dangerous?" I asked.

"Deadly, for anyone but Croom. He's been here forever. Signs up for a new tour every year. Used to be an Air Commando and go out hunting VC to slit open. They can't kill him."

"He sounds crazy," I said and wished I hadn't.

But Lebowitz, taking the stairs two at a time, called back cheerfully, "Oh, he is, he is."

Inside, the bunker was stale with dust and sweat and old vomit. I could see others huddled in the half-dark on benches along the walls. Lebowitz flopped down on the bench and I sat beside him. Through my shoulder I could feel his whole body trembling. That shocked me, for he had seemed so cool, so methodical, dressing upstairs in the room. Instantly I liked him better for it. I had thought the body under the bed and I were the only ones afraid.

Explosions boomed again, a rapid series of two or three farther away on the base. The concussions overrode the siren for a second and then it wailed shrill, piercing.

No one said anything.

A rocket slammed down close and I ducked. The blast sifted dust in streams upon us.

"Damn!" someone yelled.

I sat there squeezing my knees. Where's all that air power, I wondered. Above the siren I could hear machine gun fire and the fast-swishing beat of helicopters over the base and the roar of more Phantoms taking off. Miles away there was already the deep boom of bombs exploding.

I felt a desperate urge to run, to get away, to protect my soap-bubble body. I could smell the rancid odor of someone's gas and hoped it wasn't mine.

"All right, which coward farted?"

"Eat it, Malatesta," someone said. It was Berrigan, whose voice had told Shackler to shut up a few hours ago.

Tentative laughter, like the opening grasps in a match.

"You'd shake, too," Berrigan said, "if you were short. And me with eleven fuckin' days."

The one called Malatesta faked a loud yawn.

"Wish I had only eleven days," someone else said. "One eighty-nine and a wake up. Wait! What time is it?"

"Little after three," someone said.

"Make that one eighty-eight and a wake up."

"It all counts toward DEROS," a voice said.

The Date of Earliest Return from Overseas, the end of a man's tour. Everything was so new to me my own fear seemed irrelevant. I felt like an intruder sitting down in the last minutes of a thriller, reluctant to ask what went on in the first few reels. How did guys like Lebowitz and Tydings know so much about war, which suddenly seemed the way the real world was? Some historian. I felt like the newest babe in the woods. How do you win a war? Who was shooting rockets at us, from where? Who was out trying to stop them, and how? What happens if they start pounding us with thousands of rockets a day? *Rich*, Lebowitz called the sound. The thought of them could drive a man insane.

The voice rang out of nowhere, resonant, almost cheerful. "You cats got a woman in there?"

"Yeah," Berrigan said. "Want a piece?"

I could hear laughing just outside the tunnel.

"Croom!" Lebowitz called, his voice shrill. "Get in here before they blow your black head off."

I leaned forward but couldn't see him.

"No way," he answered.

"Dumb bastard," the one called Shackler said. "You been out on the perimeter again?"

"Take Lieutenant Hassan with you?" Berrigan called.

Croom entered the bunker and stood massive in the shaft of moonlight. The sheer bulk of the man stunned me. Croom laughed. Slowly, looming in darkness like Samson about to destroy the temple, he raised his huge arms and pressed against both sides of the tunnel.

"Nice place you have here," he said amiably. He looked slowly toward each of us, testing the walls. "Did I ever tell you guys about Tet a few years ago? They threw hundreds of those 122s in night after night. We had this big bunker with forty or fifty guys in it, see. Cats thought they were safe, bunkered down and safe. But a 122 slammed in with a delayed fuse and went through this guy's chest. Pinned him to the wall with his guts and three feet of rocket sticking out at them. It took a few seconds before they started mashing out of there yelling 'Delayed, delayed!' And then it blew. Got 'em all but two or three. I was the first one there. What a mess."

No one said anything. It was the strangest feeling, like everything else tonight. I looked up at the beamed ceiling supporting the heavy layers of sandbags and felt suddenly entombed. The siren wailed.

"Crazy bastard," Shackler growled under his breath. "So what if it happened once? Not one guy in a thousand ever gets a scratch in Nam. We're safer here than on a freeway back home."

Nine hundred ninety-nine guys out of a thousand seemed to say that.

"Lebowitz," Croom said. "Get your ass outside and let's rap."

"Can't," Lebowitz answered. "I'm on alert at 0600. Maybe Moose will."

"Who?"

"Little Moose. Our new roommate."

Lebowitz nudged me and I shook my head and said no. I might never sleep again, but if these attacks went on every night, I knew I had to get some rest.

"He says not tonight," Lebowitz called.

Croom didn't answer, merely turned and left.

After a while the siren wavered, cut out briefly and began to die. There wasn't a sound anywhere except for breathing. Lebowitz stood up. There was more bombing in the distance and soon another helicopter beat into our hearing.

The one called Berrigan went to the tunnel and peered out. "Croom?" he shouted. "Have they given the all-clear?"

There was no answer, only the helicopter louder and overwhelming, directly overhead. Then it was gone.

"Croom! Is it clear, yet?"

"Let's go," Lebowitz said to me.

Another chopper pounded overhead as we climbed the stairs. Inside, Croom lay on his bunk in shadows, silent, face to the wall.

I crossed the room and lay down, gathering my sheet from the floor. I lay awake and heard Lebowitz tossing, his bed springing tight and restless like his voice. Hooker was still under his bed.

I wondered what I could say in a report about rocket attacks. I wondered how they knew that would be all the rockets for tonight. I thought about what would happen in case of a direct hit after we fell asleep.

CROOM

The smell of fresh coffee. With my eyes closed, I sniffed for perfume. Nothing. Sheila, where are you? The bed was hard and narrow.

I opened my eyes and saw him propped up in bed across the room, staring at me. His dark wide-set eyes were deep under long hooded brows. His black short hair was curly, almost kinky. His face was evil and massive, sinisterly handsome, tanned like bull hides.

He raised a tiny china cup to his lips and sipped. He wore a trim Clark Gable mustache over wide lips, and when he grinned his teeth were bright and prominently even.

"Al Croom," he said, toasting me with the cup. "You the Little Moose?"

I raised to an elbow and nodded.

"Coffee?" he asked, and swung his feet to the floor. In the light of dawn he seemed even larger than in the bunker. He crossed slowly to the percolator on Lebowitz's chest of drawers.

Lebowitz was gone, his bunk tidy. I remembered he was on alert. The one called Hooker was also gone.

Croom offered the steaming cup and I swung upright to take it. He towered over me, grinning, sizing me up. Not the way some big men react, knowing the cocky reputation of little guys like me. I had the feeling Croom knew exactly what he was and didn't have a weak spot anywhere.

Grinning, he went slowly back to his bunk and I watched his dark body glisten powerfully. The guy had to be a tackle, at least. I wondered what Shackler had against him, except that he was crazy.

Croom raised his cup. "Lebowitz says you're here to see the war."

I nodded again. "Any suggestions?"

He closed his eyes and shrugged. "Whatever turns you on."

"Colonel Tydings wants me to see it all," I said.

Croom held up his hand. "Wait, let me guess. 'Just tell it like it is.' Right?"

I nodded and Croom laughed quietly, shaking his head.

"That Tydings," Croom said. "He's something else."

He sipped his coffee. "No one sees it all," he said. "So pick a spot. Everybody thinks he's an expert on war."

Croom finished his cup, measuring me over the rim. "Let's get breakfast," he said, standing up. "We'll start at the briefings. Everybody's an expert. You'll see what I mean."

After breakfast, we walked to headquarters with people overtaking us, splitting to pass and striding swiftly ahead. Croom walked easily, hardly moving his hands, a relaxed indifferent gait that led us into the building just before the doors were closed and locked.

We sat near the back by a major with gray hair and a twitching shoulder.

"Hooker," Croom said, "this is the Little Moose. Our new roommate. He's here to do a *SNOW* job, but don't hold that against him."

The major's brows arched over his pale eyes and he nodded. We reached across Croom to shake hands.

"Hooker's the civic action type here," Croom said.

"I couldn't do a thing without Croom," Hooker said, his deep voice dry and scratchy with smoke.

Croom shrugged. "Sometimes when I'm bored I help him out."

The tag on his chest read Major Horace Hooker. He had a broad furrowed face like a forest ranger I had met as a kid. His right shoulder kept twitching and I must have been staring at it, for he nodded, crow's feet wrinkling the edges of his eyes. He smoked with one arm supporting the other, the fingers of the hand twitching at the skin of his elbow. I wondered how a man that nervous could function at all.

Someone called "Attennn-hut!" and all officers jumped to their feet.

Colonel Bobby Dodd, the wing commander, strode in from a private office at the front, shadowed briskly by three staff officers. My boss Colonel Tydings and the civilian named Powell followed them. The civilian slouched, carrying a worn black bag, a lewd indifference about his posture. Someone yelled "Seats!" and the briefings began.

As they dragged on, they seemed like duplicates of the ones I had heard recently in Saigon. Facts about enemy activity in the South, number of missions flown, status of the force today. I began to see why Croom called everyone an expert. Green as I was, already I could spot the cynical smirk of men who have repeated certain things so often that, having said them, they think they're qualified in all related areas.

Glancing around at the hundred old heads in the room, I saw it in others, also. At the mention of new missile sites around Haiphong, Major Shackler, two rows ahead, turned knowingly to the officer on his left, nodded his head and smiled. When another briefing officer mentioned the latest Communist demands at the Paris peace talks, I saw heads shake in outraged disbelief. Through it all, Colonel Tydings sat easy in a leather armchair on the platform, a pleased smile on his face.

Looking at him was like seeing myself twenty years from now. Five-six, a bit too broad-shouldered as if he also had wrestled, he had a smaller head than mine but the same dark hair and whisker shadow, the same high cheekbones and full jaw. Handsome devil. I have one ear larger than the other, though. Hurt it wrestling, I had told Sheila.

Tydings was no wrestler. Black belt, he claimed, ever since Korea, when he was a new lieutenant like me. The founder of *SNOW*, he once had forty officers writing the history of the air war in Vietnam. But now there were only two or three others like me. The others had gone home, like all but a few thousand troops waiting for the truce at any minute.

Conceived as the ultimate white paper on the air war, *SNOW* had piled up and up like a glacier. *Successively Numbered Observations on War*. You'd think they would have run out of numbers by now. And in a year I was expected to add a few more authoritative texts? All I knew about war was what I had read in a library. A tag-team match or two hours with Sheila was enough violence for me.

Now, another officer reported on the ABF, attack by fire, last night, and I was shocked. Only one airman killed and two wounded from the first rockets, and about four or five Vietnamese killed in the second barrage that hit the crowded shacks on the edge of the base. I had expected dozens dead.

At last, Colonel Dodd drew himself suddenly to attention, head back, jaw thrust, eyes sweeping the squadron as if for MiGs. He approached the podium, locked his hands behind him, and continued scanning the room. All sat rigid, all bound. All but Croom, beside me, laughing silently. I could feel him shaking on and on, hardly pausing for breath.

Croom punched my arm. "Now listen to this cat," he said aloud.

The officer by Major Shackler looked around, his sloped head swiveling like a turtle's, close-set eyes pinching disapproval back at us.

"Eat it, Malatesta," Croom said in the same easy unmalicious voice.

The narrowed eyes stared as if checking us for loyalty. Finally, Malatesta's squat head rotated forward, scowling until his eyes panned out of range.

Colonel Dodd stood posed, immaculate in a pressed flight suit, the polished Command wings, larger than standard, gleaming on his chest. He had them torched and burnished from the twisted rocket that destroyed his hangar at Da Nang on his first tour in 1968. He wore them fiercely in the photographs I had seen of him in magazines. They were his trademark, his brand of defiance above all the air medals and his Purple Heart.

Colonel Dodd began slowly, his deep voice mellow with pride. "The new steel-reinforced revetments have been completed and now provide maximum protection for all aircraft. Guards have been doubled around them. This, despite the fact that four more ground crews departed last night for the Philippines."

He lifted a glass of water and drank from it slowly, his eyes sweeping the squadron.

He set the glass down and brushed his upper lip. "So it's up to us. We won't be getting anymore replacements." He paused, his jaw thrusting, his flared mustache riding high.

He turned slowly to acknowledge Colonel Tydings, who smiled back at him.

"You men have met Colonel Jack Tydings before," Colonel Dodd went on, his voice husky, ominous. "Most of what he briefed me on last night you're already well aware of. You know the enemy's massing troops for attacks on I Corps villages." He bit off the words, his eyes flashing.

"Whatever," he went on. "They'll have to fight for every inch of jungle right up to the last minute. If they can't control it, they'll try to destroy."

He paused and glanced around the room. "Thus the little disturbances these last few nights."

Nervous, appreciative laughter rang out, too loud.

"You've seen it—increased activity down the Ho Chi Minh Trail. They've pulled the cork out of Asia. Stuff is pouring down out of the North. And here we sit with fewer and fewer crews, and Saigon frags fewer bombing missions for us along the Trail each week."

Colonel Tydings nodded, smiling.

"Therefore, gentlemen," Colonel Dodd boomed out. "This part of the world is in for it. Bu Cai, the Special Forces camp to the west, is ready for a final assault anytime, and we should expect the same for the village of Bien Dien. We're being hit every night with just enough to keep us awake. But don't let it bother you. There's worse to come."

He scanned every face and waited. I didn't want to think about it, but I could see them—trucks and wagons bumper to bumper on the Ho Chi Minh Trail, and skinny little men no taller than me lugging rockets through the jungle, converging like doom on Bien Dien. On me. Me, who marched with Mailer on the Pentagon to try to end this lousy war. I could see myself splattered over Asia, bits and pieces blown to the winds by one of those rockets on its way down through the jungle, maybe the last rocket before the truce. I could see Sheila back home in Indiana smiling peacefully at the head-line: *All Quiet on the Eastern Front.*

Colonel Dodd raised himself on tiptoes, swaggering behind the podium. "Now here's what's new. Colonel Tydings says he has it from his 'usually reliable sources' that this year will make the Tet of '68 look tame. Word has reached the North that we're the last American fighter base, so they're sending some major fire our way. They think they can totally wipe us out. So get ready for six thousand rockets and mortars a night. "

Someone near the front started to laugh and then stopped, almost a scream, and everyone turned to his neighbor and the room shuddered with chatter. I glanced at Croom and he was simply smiling, his mustache rigid. God, I thought. There's no way.

Colonel Dodd waited a moment and then flung up his arms for silence. "Now listen! With a force of just under four hun-dred, things here could start to get sticky. Keep cool. They may be bluffing—they usually are. Bunker down at night. Sleep there, if you feel the need. But rockets are random, remember. They're not aimed, they're pointed. Their biggest damage is surprise, and we're over that, now."

He lowered his voice and looked slowly around the room at everyone. "Now you know." He pushed himself tall, inspecting us once more behind the podium. "Dismissed!"

A major leaped to his feet and yelled, "Atten-hut!"

We all jumped with him, banging our boots together. All but Croom, and Hooker. I caught Croom out of the corner of my eye slowly rising up to full height, grinning down at me. And turning my head I could see his teeth gleaming like marble, his dark eyes years beyond me. Hooker looked like a man in shock, shoulder twitching, mouth open, one eyelid fluttering. I felt desperately like a cherry boy, taken in, as if now in spite of myself I had to go out and kill someone to save my own skin, or hope somebody would.

≣THE SEND-OFF≣

Now I knew how Eddy felt. The first time I saw him I thought, poor kid, what a cherry. But after the rockets last night, I felt like nothing but a kid from the Midwest myself, staring death in the face the first time in my life. I remember the 707 touching down somewhere in Iowa—Des Moines, maybe. Inside, the green airliner from Chicago was like a mausoleum, quiet and cool. First-class eyes stared at Eddy passing by, and a stewardess glanced at his ticket.

"Two more rows," she said and hurried away.

The young airman nodded and threaded his way down the aisle past a soldier I had seen staring grimly ahead and other passengers isolated by the padded high-backed seats.

Eddy hesitated as the blonde across the aisle from me went on flipping through *Time*, her sable coat draping the aisle seat. He bent down, clutching his flight bag and his cap.

"Miss?" he said, almost a whisper.

The blonde rolled her eyes up from the magazine and stared. She was a hard thirty, still in a black evening gown and a tired face blanched with sleep.

"Excuse me?" Eddy asked, glancing at the window seat. In his blue uniform after running, he wiped at drops breaking from his hairline.

Her crossed satin legs drew in, and he stretched awkwardly across and fell.

A man across the aisle grinned at Eddy and at the blonde and settled slowly back in his seat.

She turned quietly to Eddy. "You pilots," she said, half dreaming. "So shy."

He drew his feet together. "I'm not a pilot," he said, his lips

25

tightening. A scowl like that on another man would have looked dangerous, but not on Eddy. Eddy was red haired and freckled and looked about seventeen. Kids since the first grade must have teased him about that scowl.

The air near her was thick with smoke. She stared at him, then turned slowly all the way around at me, as if she couldn't believe what she saw. Her eyes were becalmed, the pupils huge. Her lower lip was creased deep as if it had been recently split.

"I'm just out of basic training," he said. "And radar school."

"Oh, my," she said, her lips pursing. "I'll bet that was rough."

Eddy shrugged. "Naw. Not so rough." Her eyes went over his uniform and his new stripe, and he flushed.

He leaned forward to the window. I could see the people—maybe his mother and sister and maybe his Aunt Ethel from Davenport or Rapid City, at the gate, searching for him. His jaw tightened and his hand lashed up and waved at them. A girl jumped up and down and I could see the braces on her teeth as she pointed. Then the woman who must have been Eddy's mother found him. In black from someone's funeral—probably the reason he was home on leave—she dropped her handkerchief and stooped for it and all the time kept waving and trying to smile.

"Family?" the blonde asked, and he nodded and sat staring ahead.

Airborne, Eddy pulled a paperback war novel from his flight bag, and the blonde lit a Salem. Eddy leaned back, maybe relieved at last to feel the isolation he had needed. All year, ever since he joined up to get it over, his family probably had mourned as if he were dead.

Eddy crossed his legs and opened the novel.

Without warning, the blonde slipped it away from him.

"Here," a man across the aisle called, and caught it.

"Come on," Eddy said, his freckles darkening.

The man looked at the book, his dry face tight and porous like a bone, then dropped it at his side and grinned at the blonde.

"The military's going soft," he said, his voice rasping. "That book's about draft dodgers."

The blonde smiled and leaned toward Eddy. "Going to Denver?" she asked. "San Francisco?"

Eddy shook his head. "Vietnam."

"Oooh, I thought so," she said. Her eyes were like shimmering black holes. "But aren't all the troops coming home?"

"Not the Air Force," Eddy shrugged. "Not yet." He tried to grin, but gave up.

"I'm Coreen," she said, her orange lips wet. "What's your name?"

"Eddy Tivis," he said, little more than a whisper.

"Tivis," she said, and kissed him.

"Cut it out," he said. Eddy stared at the man across the aisle, who leered at them. "People are watching," Eddy said, and pulled away.

"Only him," Coreen said.

The plane lurched suddenly through turbulence, and Eddy struggled out into the aisle.

She coaxed him back with her fingers. "Just giving you a little send-off," she said.

He looked at the man with his book. Slouched, the man watched Eddy with a wry, curiously patient grin as if he thought Eddy should recognize him from somewhere. I could see his face between the split seats, one tilted back with someone sleeping. Bald on the front, he was a thin man much taller than Eddy. The skin on his face was tight like a yellowed lampshade, and he munched something behind dark lips creased with deep vertical scars.

The blonde beckoned again, her lips glistening, and Eddy retreated down the aisle to the rest room. She leaned sideways and laughed with the man across the aisle.

Eddy disappeared into the rest room and snapped the lock.

When Eddy returned, the man had moved across the aisle, and he and Coreen were leaning together, sipping drinks. Up the aisle, a stewardess bent over, serving others.

"Here, Eddy," the man invited.

Eddy hesitated. He glanced back at me as if asking for advice. His eyes were green and wide, and he was about my height, like a kid brother I never had. But he reached for both seats, then brushed over Coreen's legs and paused, having to step high over a black bag which the man guarded between his feet. A little larger than a bowling bag, it was wrinkled and cracked from long use.

Settled, Eddy glanced for his book, and the man grinned at him. His lips, wrinkled like stitches, swelled over gums crammed full of teeth.

The man took out a flask. "Want some pain killer?" he asked, and Eddy shook his head.

Soon the engines eased back and the plane descended. Coreen touched up her makeup and I thought she would get off at Denver, but she settled back in her fur and laughed at something the man said, and the plane landed and took off for San Francisco before either of them spoke to Eddy again.

Airborne, the man reached down for the book, I thought, but instead pulled out a gray pouch for a pinch of snuff, curling it under his lower lip.

"Want some?" he asked Eddy. "It's an ancient sedative, better than cigarettes." It smelled sweet and heavy and even bitter.

Eddy shook his head, and the man settled deep in the seat, watching him.

"So it caught up with you," he said, his voice flat but strangely intimate.

Eddy frowned.

"Vietnam," the man said.

"Oh." Eddy nodded.

The man sucked, his lips caressing the snuff. "Aren't many of you left over there, now." I listened as much as Eddy did.

Coreen leaned sideways in the seat, shaping her orange nails.

"Scared?" the man pumped.

Eddy shrugged, his eyes flicking from the window to the floor.

"Don't worry about it," the man said. "When they get you, they get you."

Leaning closer, the man confided, "I've been there twelve years. I was at Da Nang when a 122 rocket hit a bunker with forty guys crammed in it." Snuff began to show at the corners of his mouth, oozing also at the vertical creases that were like scars all along the lips. "I was one of the first ones there. What a mess."

The man bent between his legs and opened the black bag, slipping his hand in and out for a mug, green and waxy like pure jade. He lifted it to his lips and spat.

Coreen put away her file, smoothed her gown over her thighs, and leaned back. The man turned toward her and then, as an afterthought, extended his hand to Eddy.

"My name's Powell," he said. "Vince Powell."

He leaned back and turned to the woman, leaving Eddy upright by the window. Eddy stared out but we were in the clouds, still climbing.

I'm sure he was scared. All the time growing up, he must have played war, like me, with pals named Billy and Paul, and mowed lawns for money to see war movies and westerns. That was an excitement like nothing else, a nobility in being the good guys with everything at stake, and winning. But then they turned eighteen, and Paul or Billy went off to Vietnam and the war games they played as kids were back again, but not for fun.

I had a buddy like that, Freddy Dwyer. Freddy shipped over as a helicopter gunner. He was tough, five-ten and not afraid of anything. For a year I carried in my wallet a picture of Freddy in his flak vest, his camouflaged flight suit creased and his new mustache full and neat, an Australian bush hat cocked jauntily on his head and winking his "go-get-'em" smile from Da Nang. The day Freddy left, I read for hours about Vietnam, and found a map of the country in *National Geographic* and taped it to my bedroom door. Years later when Sheila saw it, she peeled the dry tape loose, took the map to the sink, and burned it.

After he had been there only a few months, Freddy's letters began to go sour. One day, an officer stopped by to tell Freddy's father about the crash. At the funeral, the church was only a fourth full, so late in the war. Freddy's death seemed almost irrelevant, with the newspapers telling daily of more and more units coming home. At the closed-casket funeral, five other friends and I had borne the flag-draped coffin, which was strangely heavy. For rumor had it that there was no body.

For an hour, Eddy kept his face to the window of the airplane, and I looked out to see the sunset. We were out of the clouds, now, and off to the north I could see mountains, dark and lustrous at the tops, violet and dark purple, stretching away in deepening nighttime shadows. Probably like Eddy's, my throat was tight with mixed emotions. It was a beautiful country, and I loved it. The grandeur of the West was just what I thought it would be. The mountains were like scenes in movies, and this seemed like the climax of a movie approaching, an orchestra from balcony speakers in my mind swelling "America the Beautiful" as the wide camera panned downrange toward the Golden Gate, and for a time I felt part of a terrible national drama.

"Kid," Vince Powell said. "Eddy."

Eddy sat up and glanced sideways, blinking.

"It's nothing to be ashamed of," Powell said. "Everybody's scared sometimes."

"No, I . . ."

"Relax."

The blonde stared at him, her lips cracked in a contented smile. The man's eyes were squinted almost shut, and the creases of his mouth oozed rivulets of snuff like blood, as if his lips had been stitched.

Eddy stared at him, blinking. Powell's face, especially the lips, reminded me of something we were told in training. Always stay together, the sergeants warned. If any fools get lost and captured, the VC would cut off their balls, stuff them in their mouth and sew up the lips, then cut off their head and impale it on a post in the nearest village.

Powell raised the back of his seat even with Eddy's.

"Why have you stayed in Nam so long?" I heard Eddy ask as he stared at the man's face.

Powell lifted his jade cup and spat snuff juice quietly. "It's my job."

"But you're a civilian. You don't have to stay there."

Powell shrugged. "I can get more work there than in the States." He leaned nearer. "I'm head of CISCO. Ever hear of us?"

Eddy shook his head.

"You will," Powell said. "Casualty investigating team."

Eddy seemed to be having to think to breathe. "Not many guys get killed there," Eddy said. "Do they?"

"Naw. Fewer and fewer." Powell tapped his arm. "What's your job?"

"Radar," Eddy said, as if not sure if he was supposed to tell. "The 259th."

Powell's eyes widened, and he lifted the cup to his mouth. "Who'd you have to kill to get that?"

Eddy leaned back. "Good duty, huh?"

Powell broke into a fit of coughing and held his other hand over the mug. Sighing, he drew out his handkerchief and wiped his lips. "Well," he said. "Now, that depends on if you mind being alone or not."

"I don't mind," Eddy shrugged.

Powell studied him, his eyes blank. "You'd better not. You'll be in a shack out on a hilltop west of Da Nang with nothing around but jungle and Victor Charlies." He shook his head. "How old are you, Eddy?"

"Nineteen."

Powell looked off toward the front of the cabin. "The fellow I just brought back was twenty-nine." He wiped his lips again. "Someone has to fly home with the bodies, see, so I take one out every three, four months. Gets me a little holiday, now and then. This last fellow was a military historian. You know, going around for the Air Force, writing up the air war. I ran into him once over at Pleiku. Last week he was at the 253rd—a radar shack like yours, over near the Ho Chi Minh Trail. They cut him down coming off the mountain on his way back to Saigon."

I stared at the black case between Powell's feet. I thought of a horror movie from childhood about a sinister figure who followed victims marked for decapitation, and who carried a black bag for their heads.

"They're always doing that," Powell mused.

"What?" Eddy asked quietly.

"Ambushing radar sites. If they make up their minds to take one, it's all over."

"What about help from air strikes?" Eddy said, his voice empty.

Powell cleaned his lips with the stained handkerchief. "For what? All they can do is blow the top of the hill off. Look, they've got pictures of one site being overrun. The VC made it look easy. All the pilot could do was circle and take pictures and waste several thousand rounds in the jungle. When he was sure the last friendly was dead, he blew the radar to hell and returned to his base."

Eddy sat for a while, his eyes to the floor, breathing long and deep. Slowly, he inched his way up by clutching the seat in front of him.

"Gotta go to the bathroom," he said.

Powell pointed to the front. "Too late," he said, indicating the seat-belt light. "We're already landing at San Francisco."

The blonde left without a word, but Powell waited in the aisle with his bag. Slowly, I followed him and Eddy off the plane and into the long corridor of the terminal.

Inside the vast lobby with shops and motor carts and people with bright clothes hurrying everywhere, Powell stopped and held out his hand, thin and limp like a skeleton's.

"I leave you here," he said, and glanced at me for the first time. "Staying over for a couple of days."

He dug Eddy's book from his coat pocket. "Here. Some fellows use books like these to raise their bunks with. Easier to slip under when the rockets start crashing in."

Powell grinned. "But listen, where you're going, don't worry about it."

Eddy took the book and looked helplessly around. "Where do I go now?"

Powell pointed to a counter with an Army sergeant behind it. "He'll tell you what to do next."

I was glad I waited, relieved that I also knew now what to do.

Eddy stared at Powell, his lips tight, his face burning. He seemed lost, as if even such a small task as finding his way to Travis Air Force Base for his flight overseas seemed impossible to him.

"What do I . . .?" His tongue clicked dry.

Powell lay his hand familiarly on Eddy's back and nudged. Eddy went forward a few steps, stopped and looked back. Nodding, Powell raised his hand again.

"I'll see you, Eddy," he said, his eyes hollow, his voice soft. "See you sometime in Nam."

THE TRACK

By noon Bien Dien sweltered, the humid air heavy like deep depression. The clouds had not built far enough to block out the sun, which beat down almost too bright to see. For the first time since the rocket blast last night, the base was quiet, as if totally shut down. I could not hear a jet or bombs or gunfire anywhere. The whole war seemed to have been called off.

I felt my back baking already as Lebowitz guided me, jogging the three blocks to the track, a dirt oval bulldozed around a field laid out for football but covered now in dead yellow grass, a collapsing rusting goalpost at each end. Lebowitz said that in the old days, with a half million Americans in Vietnam, the base was famous as Bien Dien-by-the-Sea, its beaches a favorite R and R center. But after most of the troops were withdrawn, there weren't enough left for proper patrols, and the VC began mining the beaches. Now the ocean was off limits, and jogging was the best hot way to relax.

A road paralleled the track and cut north to the flight line a few blocks away, hidden by hangars and Quonset huts. Along the other side of the field were wooden bleachers built between the forty-yard lines, a platform at the fifty like a parade reviewing stand. Behind the bleachers a sagging cyclone fence ran the length of the field, and on the other side were rows and rows of tin and wooden shacks where Vietnamese airmen lived with their families. And at the far end of the field, beyond a great wall smothered with vines, there was a huge French mansion with a red roof and trees everywhere around it, like part of the jungle.

There were a dozen or more men in trunks already on the track, some of them jogging fast, some shuffling along with

34

their heads down, their arms hanging. Lebowitz drew the
towel from his neck and wiped his face and threw the towel
on the field. His thin face was drawn, and his eyes had that
haunted, hollow stare from dark sockets, his stiff white hair
already glistening.

"Six times around for a mile," he said, not breaking stride.

"How many miles do you go?" I asked, my bones heavy in
the heat.

"Four, five, I'll let you know."

He ran light on his feet, a thin man with long muscles. He
kept his fists straight out in front of him, knuckles up. He was
taller than me by several inches, his long stride hitting three
for my four. His high voice chattered like a separate thing
that could not be winded.

"See that guy rounding the end zone? That's Fleming. He
runs every day. The only guy here who can outlast me."

"Yeah," I said, still trying to fall in with his pace. "I
see him."

Fresh from the States, I was used to handball and an indoor
track, and running in this humidity was like treading deep
water with boots on.

I watched Fleming round the turn and enter the straight-
away, running fast with determined desperate lunges past a
group of slower joggers and along the row of Vietnamese
shacks. Three children broke from the bushes and ran to
the track, whirling and darting away out of sight as Fleming
ran past. When the children broke toward the group following him, one of the men lunged at them and the children
scattered.

We approached the turn and the old wall of the French
estate towered before us, lush with vines and blossoms,
shaded by the great limbs of trees beyond the wall.

"The Frenchman's place," Lebowitz said, tossing his thumb
at the wall. "It's their private club, now."

I had read about Bien Dien before leaving Saigon. I knew

it was one of the American bases built in the sixties, bulldozed not merely out of jungle but out of an old French colonial plantation on the bay. At the peak of U.S. involvement, eighteen thousand Americans crowded the base, along with a handful of French still running their plantation and a few hundred Vietnamese. Now, only four hundred Americans remained and thousands of Vietnamese and still the handful of French, who lived apart and never troubled themselves with Americans except invitations to the base commander and his staff at Christmas and the fourth of July and Bastille Day.

I heard a board thudding just beyond the wall, and then a splash cut trimly into water.

"Swimming pool," Lebowitz said, not even glancing at the wall, his fists pumping. "Those cats still think they're in the Promised Land."

We turned down the backstretch and came even with the shacks. There was an awful smell, like rotten cabbages and vinegar.

"You numbah ten!" a child's voice screamed, the worst insult possible. "You 'mericans numbah ten!"

Lebowitz never turned his head toward that supreme insult, just kept jogging the same steady pace. And when the child screamed at us again, Lebowitz called back, friendly, "You numbah one! You numbah one, boychild!"

He answered my silence as we jogged on. "Want to trade places with them?"

"No way," I said.

"You're right," he said. "If we can't be friends with the kids, there's no way."

Shackler and Malatesta arrived from the officers' hootches, and we fell in behind them as they entered the track, jogging heavily. Shackler lunged along, leaning forward like a heavyweight, but Malatesta brought his knees high and trotted with his shoulders thrust back as if on parade.

"They hit the village again?" Lebowitz called.

"Naw," Shackler replied, not looking back. "Must be getting ready to pound the base."

Rumors. At breakfast someone had said three NVA divisions had crossed the demilitarized zone and were last seen forty kilometers north of the base. Rumors of casualties from last night's mortar and rocket attacks ran as high as dozens of Americans and hundreds of Vietnamese killed and God knows how many wounded. Someone said the VC had overrun half of Plei Nhon and massacred scores of villagers during the night.

I waited for someone else to talk, but all ran quietly, all alone. Now and then we would fall into step and there would be the thump thump thump of our running. Then the steps would syncopate and break rhythm and in the heavy depressing heat I would find myself having to concentrate to maintain stride.

Fleming caught us in the second lap and passed without looking, his breath puffing, the tendons in his neck stretched tight. He was a good-looking kid with blond hair and flushed cheeks and he looked too young to be out of high school. He raced on, as if trying to outdistance fear.

Each time we passed the wall I listened, and once I thought I heard sensual laughter, and another time I heard music, slow and light and peaceful, like Paris in springtime.

A muscular, middle-aged man ran past us, deeply tanned, an old sergeant or a colonel, his thick white hair glistening with sweat. Around his waist he wore a wide leather back support, gleaming black, a blue .38 holstered on one side and a knife scabbard stitched to the other.

"Watch him," Lebowitz said. "He won't go near the shacks."

Sure enough, the man ran swiftly along the inside of the track, next to the football field.

"Hates kids?" I asked.

"Naw," he said. "Just afraid someone's gonna nail him before it's over. He's not the only one."

After three laps Shackler and Malatesta dropped out, panting heavily, but Lebowitz jogged on, staring ahead. I glanced at them walking slowly back toward the quarters, their arms limp. I felt more like that than running, but something in my legs kept going and after a few paces I caught up with Lebowitz again.

"It all counts toward DEROS," he said grimly. Date of Earliest Return from Overseas: months, impossible months from now.

We must have jogged around that track for an hour. One by one the others dropped out and returned to the barracks for showers and back to duty. After a while there were only Lebowitz and I and, lapping us every two or three rounds, Fleming, haunting the day with his fear.

Lebowitz paced me like a record spinning around and around, lap after lap. I caught my mind wandering off the track, dozing, drugged with fatigue and the heat. I no longer heard the children jeering at us, only now and then a woman's high strange scolding from inside the shacks, or a crying baby. I listened for the swimming pool to splash again or for music, but there were not even birds singing in the Frenchman's jungle beyond the wall. After a while even Lebowitz hushed and there was only the thump of our toes jogging on dirt.

My lungs numbed in the heat and my legs came to feel like things apart, able to go on and on. My eyes burned with sweat, and I squinted so tight I could hardly see, and because they stung it was impossible to think. I was adjusting, though, lost in rhythm, like a mechanical animal going around and around, getting closer to DEROS. It felt good and I was slipping deep in dreams when I heard a noise with my name on it.

"Moose. It's time, Moose," Lebowitz called.

I jolted to a halt off the track and dropped my arms. My hands were numb. I heard jets roaring from the flight line. Drenched in sweat, tasting salt and iodine, I shuddered. It was overcast, the sky boiling with clouds, and in the distance there was thunder, or bombs, and I knew from the noon sun burning my skull there was still a long, long way to go.

MAYDAY

≡ SNOW JOB ≡

Lebowitz met me at the door.

"Come on!" he yelled, running to the flight line. "Maybe we can catch him."

"Shackler?" I shouted, jogging behind him. "He said be here by 1400."

Lebowitz ran faster. "A scramble," he yelled. "The Special Forces camp's under attack. No time to look for you."

He clamped his flight cap and ducked his head, darting behind an F-4 pulling in for shutdown. The hot blast hit us, blurring everything. The jet looked like a giant locust creeping to a halt.

We found the F-4s with Shackler already in the cockpit of one. Only his head was visible, puny in the huge Phantom, green and drab brown and heavy with napalm and rockets.

"Malatesta!" Lebowitz shouted to the man in the rear cockpit. "He's here, no thanks to you. Get your ass out!"

He turned to me. "So this is your first flight in a Phantom, Moose? Did Shackler check you out?"

I nodded. "He had Captain Malatesta take me over to Personal Equipment and brief me on the back seat."

"Good." He looked me over.

"Where's your G-suit? Where's the survival vest?"

I shrugged.

"Malatesta!" Lebowitz shouted. "You forgot his damn G-suit!"

Malatesta, unstrapped by now and climbing down, held a finger out at Lebowitz.

"Well, damn," Lebowitz said to me. "You still want to go?"

"Sure," I said, not knowing what else to do.

"All right, then, suck in your gut in a dive. And don't touch a thing. I'll check you out good tomorrow."

He pulled me to the yellow ladder high on the side of the aircraft. "Malatesta's my WSO," he said, "weapon systems operator. A West Pointer who washed out of pilot training and had to be a navigator. Pisses him off to take a back seat to anyone, but flies any time there's a rear seat open."

Malatesta jumped the last step to the tarmac and glared at me, his head squashed inside his helmet.

"Well, get in, dammit," Malatesta snapped. "He's got to go!"

I climbed the hot ladder and felt it shake as Lebowitz followed me up. The cockpit was like a spaceship's to me, black, crammed with dials and switches. The ejection seat reared like a supersonic electric chair, and I stepped down into it like a Jonah sliding into the whale's spout.

Lebowitz helped me fasten the parachute and strapped me in, all the time shouting what I must and must not do, in a high-pitched scream above the F-4 starting up next to us. I glanced over at it and saw Malatesta climbing quickly into the rear cockpit, the young WSO he had bumped standing below him on the ladder.

"I'll meet you after the flight and buy you a beer," Lebowitz shouted.

There was a parachute leg strap loose and Lebowitz took it and began flailing my leg until I grabbed his hand.

"That sting?" he yelled. "Fold it under the webbing here. If you eject at 400 knots, that strap will beat you to shreds. Hey, just relax. You'll be okay."

Shackler signaled to the ground crew and twisted around.

"Get the hell off!" he yelled at Lebowitz. He jammed his helmet on and leered at Lebowitz. "Malatesta says you shot up the village today."

"We hit a mortar site nearby," Lebowitz said, his jaw muscles working. "They were dug in near the village."

"Malatesta says you laid it right in there close." He leered again. "We'll make a killer out of you, yet."

Lebowitz said nothing, merely lifted the helmet from the canopy rail and held it over my head. He worked the helmet down over my ears and shoved and suddenly all noise ceased, all but the faint high-pitched hum of the aircraft next to us. I could more nearly feel the jet roar with my skin than hear it.

Then Lebowitz clamped the rubber oxygen mask over my face and cinched it tight. I felt a faraway rumble through my boots as Shackler started the right engine, then the left. Lebowitz banged on my helmet and yelled something, gave the thumbs-up sign and backed down the ladder.

A crewman lifted the ladder away and others ran from the plane, dragging the wheel chocks, and I became aware of radio transmissions, buzzing and thin, their meaning garbled.

Suddenly, Shackler's voice spoke to me loud and close, as if he were right behind me in a cave.

"How do you read me, Moose?"

I looked for a microphone button, but the cockpit was a scheme of dials.

"Moose?"

"Where's the mike button?" I asked, surprised to hear my own voice distant and distorted.

"It's a hot mike," Shackler's voice came back. "Just talk and I'll hear you. All set?"

"I guess so," I said, learning the meaning of blind faith.

The buzz came again and I recognized Shackler's voice calling the tower for taxi and takeoff instructions.

When the tower replied with a long rapid technical directive I couldn't follow, the F-4 started to roll, braked, and rolled again, followed by Malatesta and the pilot in the number two aircraft.

While we taxied out to the runway, bumping brittle and heavy over the concrete, I glanced around at the maze of instruments, careful to keep my palms flat on my thighs. I recognized a radar scope and some of the basic flight instruments, altimeter, airspeed Mach indicator, and others less familiar. Most of the cockpit, though, was like the lab of a mad scientist, rigged to explode.

Shackler stopped in the arming area just off the runway, where ground crewmen ducked underneath to remove the safety wires from the ordinance. They emerged with the wires, tagged with red flags, and the crew chief gave Shackler thumbs-up.

Then Shackler lined us up on the runway and braked to a halt. The other Phantom stopped alongside, dangerously close to our wing, it seemed to me.

"Duke flight," Shackler called, "go button three."

I heard the radio whirring, then Shackler's voice, "Duke Lead on three."

"Duke Two," the other pilot acknowledged.

"Bien Dien Tower, Duke Flight ready for takeoff."

"Roger, Duke. Cleared for takeoff on runway three-zero, wind two-three-zero at five. Contact departure control after takeoff."

"Roger, tower."

The engines began to wind up toward takeoff power. The aircraft, locked by brakes, took hold of the runway, shuddered with the blast of the engines, grabbed hard, hard, and released.

I felt myself go back, sagging into the back support, every ounce of meat welding to the solid frame of the Phantom hurtling faster and faster down the runway. It launched suddenly into the air, amazingly swift and silent, the concrete falling desperately away beneath us. I had never felt such speed. The runway and buildings disappeared, the green jungle fell rapidly away into a richer deeper green, and the aircraft banked steeply around to the west.

I looked above us in the left turn. The other F-4, big as a

barn, hovered directly overhead, clinging there in the sky. It seemed it would have to fall into us and crash. But I could see the pilot dwarfed in the cockpit, his dark sun visor shielding his eyes, watching us, flying beautiful formation.

I wondered how in the world Colonel Tydings expected me to record a combat mission. Most of the time I didn't know what was going on. After we banked west in the climb-out, I lost my sense of direction and listened in dumb wonder at the radio transmissions, almost totally cryptic, the private jargon of fighter pilots.

Throughout the flight, like a child I watched in puzzled rapture the strange discoveries happening to my body. I stretched in the cockpit, straining to see, forgetting how to find the switch to raise the seat higher. In the turns, foreign pressures molded my body. When Shackler dumped the stick forward, I felt alien, detached from earth, shoved awkwardly against the shoulder harness.

Now and then Shackler tossed bits of information back to me, although not very concerned with whether I learned. Or maybe it hadn't occurred to him how new I really was.

"Bu Cai's taking some heavy stuff," he would say, his voice loud and calm in my ears. Always between transmissions he would hum to himself.

And I would have to ask, "What's Bu Cai? Is that the Special Forces camp?"

After he finished humming a verse he would reply, "That's affirmative. Twenty more klicks to the west."

And I would wait, hearing him hum.

"What's happening to them?" I would ask, finally, feeling like an intruder, a fool.

"A little action," he'd say, humming.

"Heavy attack?"

"Hummm?"

"Is it a heavy attack?"

Seldom a straight answer from Shackler. Humming.

When he winged over and started down, I saw the camp laid out in the jungle, barricaded like a Boy Scout excursion between two mountains, a road winding off for miles down the valley to the south. From altitude the camp appeared to be at the bottom of the valley, but as we dived down deeper, deeper beneath the scattered clouds and then plunged below the mountain tops, I saw that the camp was actually on a plateau, a bleak meadow with rows of huts like a tenement section.

Diving, we swooped over the meadow and on into the dark valley. I saw an OV-10 spotter plane circling out to the right and the smoke where he had marked a target with smoke rockets.

"Cricket 23, Duke Flight," Shackler called the Forward Air Controller. "Two F-4s, rockets, guns, and napalm. What you need?"

"Roger, Duke. Attack's been driven back. For now, just have some troop trucks and probably supplies pegged in that wooded section just north of my northernmost smoke. How about a few rockets and a little nape? They're all yours."

"Roger, Cricket," Shackler called. "We'll make a rocket pass first and nape 'em the second time around. Randy, take your spacing and let's work a wagon wheel to the right."

"Roger, Lead—spacing and wagon wheel right."

"That's affirm," Shackler said.

Hurtling from the sky, nearer, nearer the green earth, we dived again, in and out of the valley in seconds that seemed like forever, the dials spinning crazily. I felt my feet clutch inside my boots, straining against the floor as thin smoke spiraled up from the jungle. I felt chained to a twenty-ton meteor hurtling at the earth. Then the rockets thrust forward ahead of us faster than I thought rockets could go, and the nose of the aircraft jerked up and I slammed suddenly into blackout, without sensation, like dying in my sleep.

After that, I tried to anticipate the pullout and grab my breath hard, slowing the blood flow from my upper body. I grayed out, but never completely lost sight of the cockpit again. I would hate to have been flying the plane. How Shackler, fat and forty and casually humming Johnny Cash, kept us in the air, I didn't know.

After another pass, Shackler contacted the FAC again. "Too much foliage to be sure, Cricket. A couple of the trucks are exposed, though. How many you figure are down there?"

"Estimate eight or ten, Duke."

"Roger, Cricket. Randy, let's try some more napalm on those two trucks sticking out at the west end of the trees. Maybe we can spread the fire around a little. Lead heading in from the west at five hundred feet for a shallow drop."

"Roger, Lead. Sounds good."

On the third pass I looked back and saw fire bursting in the trees. I hadn't felt the napalm release, and I felt detached from the jellied flames, absolved, as if someone behind us had dropped them. An impersonal feeling. I had felt worse about such bombings on TV a year ago, half a world away.

Then we were above the clouds, still climbing, with Shackler humming and the dials spinning and no one had even fired at us. I couldn't believe it was over so soon. I thought to myself, well, if they can teach monkeys to fly maybe I could learn, too. I wiped the sweat off my palms. Flying combat wasn't so bad.

I couldn't tell if we had hit anything or not. The FAC assessed the battle damage as eighty percent target coverage with rockets and napalm, two trucks destroyed and three probably damaged, but from the way Shackler muttered "Damn" I knew he thought he had hit more than that. He soon seemed happy enough, though, humming "A Boy Named Sue" like deep static.

I hadn't thought once about the soldiers and natives in the Special Forces camp we came here to save. I discovered with a twinge of conscience that they didn't really exist for me, vulnerable as I had been. That they had been attacked and that we might have helped them for a few hours meant little more than reports I had been reading for days. They were men and they would someday die, and the sky overhead was indifferently blue, and suddenly again I felt useless as tits on a boar hog.

"Randy," Shackler called. "Take any hits?"

The other pilot answered, "A couple, I guess. No sweat."

Humming, Shackler twisted to look over his left shoulder. "I'm showing hydraulic fluctuation. Positive lateral control, but I suspect a leak. Look close when you check me over."

"Roger," the other pilot said.

The other F-4 slipped smoothly down and under us, stayed a moment and slid easily back up into formation, inches from our right wing.

"A couple of holes," he reported. "No leaks showing, so they might have hit a gauge."

"Roger," Shackler called. "I'll give it a check before we land. I'll look you over, now."

"Roger."

Shackler slid us down and under and the whole sky grew dark with the massive Phantom brooding lizard green only a few feet above us.

"You're clean," Shackler reported, climbing back into the lead.

Humming. Both of them so cool. I hadn't even known we were being shot at. I glanced down to be sure I hadn't been hit, thinking Moose, you're a hero. But knowing I wasn't.

"Tydings wants me to give you a peek at Bien Dien village," Shackler broke in.

"The village near the base?" I asked.

"Yeah, it's been getting hit pretty bad lately. We keep it from being overrun."

He yanked the stick and we plunged into a diving turn. I

was amazed that the other aircraft could stay with us, but there it was, only a few feet away, its wings tilted starkly against the sky.

Shackler eased off into a shallow spiral around the village, isolated, a single pocket in the deep green jungle that sprawled in all directions. The village looked gaudy in all that green, a shimmering oriental mosaic, sunlight flashing from puddle to puddle and along the stream that carved Bien Dien in half.

Clusters of trees dominated the village, with tan roofs of houses arranged like geometric designs along irregular dirt streets ending sometimes in fields a few acres across, standing half in water.

As we spiraled, light played off hundreds of shacks made of tin, the glitter gathering to thousands of brilliant flashes as we circled. Descending, I could see rubble, craters in the fields and houses flattened randomly. Some craters were old, with water standing. Others were likely from recent rocket attacks, the fresh earth red. There was a new crater in what looked like a playground or school yard, with people standing around it.

Smoke hung over the rubble in the center of the village, the glow of flames like coals from deep in the shadows. At the far end of the village, on the edge of the refugee camp, an entire section had been leveled, the earth scorched, riddled with debris like a tornado's wake.

"A direct hit?" I asked.

"Hum?"

"Right there," I said. "Did rockets do all that?"

"Right there? Naw, that's where we bombed them a couple of nights ago. Bastards slipped into the village and the ground controller called in an air strike. If he hadn't gotten there in time they'd have the whole village by now. Nuke 'em and nape 'em."

Nuke 'em and nape 'em. Nuclear war and napalm, Shackler's solution to the masses threatening our shores. If Sheila could see me now.

The spot looked deserted, a smudge at the edge of the village, and I watched it slipping away until erased by our wing.

Shackler raised the nose and thrust the throttle forward, banking sharply over the village.

"Randy," he called the other Phantom, "we'll orbit awhile. Something might turn up. Hey, Randy, meet Little Moose Mosely. Moose, that's Captain Wayne flying our wing, Captain Malatesta in the back."

In the front cockpit, Captain Wayne tossed a salute, the aircraft steady. Shackler hummed, and I watched the other F-4 climbing close and graceful on our wing, the jungle falling away beneath us, luxuriantly green, broken by patches of white clouds like bomb bursts.

"Been to jungle survival school?" Shackler asked.

"No, sir," I said.

Humming. Then he said, "Hell. Why do they let you fly?"

I shrugged, knowing he couldn't see me. But what could I say?

"Tell you what," he said between verses. "If we ever get shot down, you stick tight." I nodded.

"But not to worry," he said. "Smart fighter pilots don't get shot down."

He rolled left, as if pointing at the jungle with the wing tip. "And if you know how to survive down there, Search and Rescue can find you almost anywhere in Southeast Asia. If you know how." Humming.

I found myself watching for clearings. "Do many guys crash?"

"Naw," he said. "Not many. An occasional Golden Beebee."

"What's that?"

"A bullet or Triple-A burst with your name on it, antiaircraft fire. Or SAM, a surface-to-air-missile. You know. Fate."

"Roger," I said. Slowly, I was beginning to understand the

jargon, and it made a seductive kind of sense. Wagon wheels, nuke 'em and nape 'em, Golden Beebees. Clever sayings. What's in a name could mean the difference between fear and laughter. What they called killing over here in the air made it witty, took it out of the heart and into the cortex.

Shackler finished humming "A Boy Named Sue" and started over again.

Suddenly there was a lot of chatter on the radio and I tried to make it out.

"Did you copy that, Randy?"

A pause. "I'm not sure. Something about Pimah Mountain."

"Listen."

The chatter came again, garbled.

"Unit calling for air support, say again," Shackler called, his volume turned high.

I caught the words "Pimah Mountain" and something under attack, but it was terribly garbled, as if dozens were talking at once to someone calling for help.

"Come up guard, Randy," Shackler said, his voice brittle.

They switched to the emergency frequency and I could hear the mechanism whirring. Then guard channel tuned and I could hear the voice clearly, as close as our wing man's.

"Under attack, Mayday, Mayday," the young voice called calmly, a voice from the Midwest, "Pimah Mountain is under attack, request urgent aid. Air cover urgently needed."

Shackler broke in as he banked hard to the north. "Pimah, this is Duke Leader with two Phantoms about a hundred south. Sit tight, we're on our way."

". . . under attack, Mayday, Mayday," the voice went on with the same flat inflection, clear, without panic.

"It's a recording," Randy Wayne said gently.

"Yeah," Shackler said. "Malatesta, got a fix on it, yet?"

"Three-five-zero, for now," Malatesta called, his bent helmet barely showing in the rear cockpit. "Eighty-four nautical miles, about seven minutes."

"Let's go afterburner," Shackler called, and I watched the Mach needle climb almost to the speed of sound.

I waited until he finished humming.

"Isn't Pimah Mountain a radar site?"

"Yeah, the 259th," he said. "Ten or fifteen men sitting up on the mountain with nothing around but jungle and VC. We've lost two sites already since the monsoon. Now this one."

"Will we get there in time?"

He snorted. "Hell, they're already dead, probably. We can't save them. Once the VC and the NVA mass on a site, it's done for. Can't you tell that's a recording?"

The voice kept calling "Mayday" over and over, mechanically, with what seemed to me now fatalistic flatness. I wondered about the boy who had recorded that message for just such an eventuality. How long ago, I wondered. Was it Eddy, the kid I met on the way over to Vietnam? Was he dead, now, dying even as four miles up and seventy miles away we flew to his aid? What had he thought some time ago as he read off the prescribed doomed plea into the recorder? Like making out a will, knowing someone will hear it after you've gone.

Thus the formal wording, the dignified flatness of the message, to be played only when attacked. In that case, whoever recorded it might be safe. If someone on the first crew recorded it, he would have rotated back to the States years ago. He and I might have been classmates. He might be working for General Motors now, a rising executive.

And the poor kid born too late, or a guy who stayed out of the military as long as he could, might now be the one hiding down there, praying that the emergency measures taken by military bastards he damned while safe at home in the sixties would save him. It might even be Eddy.

Poor bastard. Here come forty tons of American aid at six hundred miles an hour and you're already as good as dead, Shackler says.

"Three minutes," Malatesta called.

I saw the throttle come back and felt myself nudged forward against the shoulder straps.

"Penetration in ten seconds," Shackler announced.

"Come right to three-five-eight degrees," Malatesta said.

Shackler realigned and dropped the nose. Then I saw the mountain directly ahead, rising out of the jungle. It rose to a mesa small and almost flat, like an ancient volcano. I tried hard to see gun smoke. I could see the radar dome and the massive reflector. They certainly hadn't made it a secret they were there. It was a wonder they hadn't been attacked before now.

"Lost the signal," Malatesta reported.

"Then they've had it," Shackler said.

The silence in the headset was hollow.

"Let's go back to channel five," Shackler said.

"Roger," Randy Wayne replied, and I heard the radio whir.

When the channel cleared, Shackler called, "See anything, Randy?"

Wayne answer, "Nothing yet."

"Spread out and back. See if they shoot at me on this first pass."

Wayne fell off behind us and Shackler started humming again. He leveled out and cocked a wing up, exposing us to their gunfire as we spiraled around the mountaintop. I could see long bunkers, mounded with sandbags throughout the compound.

The area was about the size of two or three tennis courts. There were the dome and the giant reflector and wires all over the place. Craters and debris scattered in an arc away from the dome, and as we orbited around to the other side I saw where a blast had knocked out a wall.

"Norm," Randy Wayne called. "They're shooting at you."

"Where?" Shackler asked, his helmet against the canopy.

"Behind you, now. Bend it around and I'll have a shot."

Shackler yanked up hard left and I strained against the

force. I let my head turn and saw Wayne's rockets burst a few meters down the mountain.

"I see 'em," Shackler called, "a whole company firing at us."

"They're in the bunkers, too," Wayne said.

"Let 'em have it, then."

I saw him first, a single American in fatigues, hunched like a green speck under the lip of the mesa, hiding from the soldiers that kept popping from the bunkers to fire at us.

"Look there!" Shackler said, calling out his position.

"I see him," Wayne replied. His voice showed nothing could be done.

It was only a matter of time before they would sweep the perimeter and find him hiding. I wondered if there were others or if he was the last one alive. Chances are he was alone, for as we spiraled I saw no other places to hide. There was no way to get him out, for we weren't even suppressing their fire as it was, and it would be worse when they spotted him.

But Shackler radioed a report, and we learned that Foxfire Flight was on the way, as well as rescue choppers.

I wondered if the American saw us, if he knew we couldn't help. He was still crouched against the limestone cliff. He was on a ledge about six feet below the rim, and above a sheer drop.

"Son of a bitch," Shackler said. "I bet he doesn't even have a gun with him."

Shackler made another pass and fired rockets at the huge radar reflector, shattering one side. Cables whipped wildly as we zoomed past. He racked the plane around and I could see soldiers standing up and firing at us and then ducking into bunkers as Randy Wayne began his run.

As we arched around I saw the man on the ledge standing, holding out his hand to us, a futile gesture, not a wave or a salute and not really a call for help. He must have known he was already dead. I think he was stunned to see friends still out of their reach, for it must have seemed to him the world was doomed. He might have wanted to be seen before he died.

Although he faced us, I still didn't know. It could be Eddy. But whoever he was, he was too far away, trapped on a rock. Poor bastard. He hadn't been in-country long enough to know how to die, according to Shackler, didn't even have a gun with him.

That was Shackler, man with a gun, whipping around a mountain at four hundred knots, cool as a Bloody Mary, safe and comfortable as modern aeronautics could make him. I shook my head. It dawned on me that Shackler might be closer to death than the boy on the cliff. One shot, just one Golden Beebee on a steep pass and Shackler would go down in twisting, devastating flame. And here I was, five feet behind him, and I would sizzle and smash from the same bullet that had his name on it.

How in the hell did I get here, I wondered, tandem to a man too bold to be afraid? What he was doing with our bodies was obscene. Why expose ourselves to thousands of rounds of gunfire if nothing could be done for that soldier? I felt like a buzzard, hovering overhead, waiting for him to die. If there were any chance to save him, if I were in his shoes, surely any risk would be worth it. Maybe he was waving us away, maybe he knew the risk and was warning us to back off, to save ourselves.

But on the next, lower pass he watched us hurtle by, crouched, his hands hugging the cliff. Poor devil. We flew by so close I could see his face. I knew him. I really did.

Frozen there, a fixed point almost blurred as we whirled past, he looked calm, now, almost at peace, like a corpse ready for burial, past all human endeavor, past all the scowls and pity of the living who circled helplessly overhead to pay their last respects, hurtling toward our own inevitable fates.

"Uh, oh," Shackler said. "They've found him."

I leaned forward and sure enough, several of the men in

black a hundred feet below the ledge had seen him. They began to shoot.

"Get 'em, Randy," Shackler said, bending the F-4 up and around.

There was a pause and then a calm, "My gun's dry," from Wayne.

"Damn," Shackler muttered on intercom. He tightened the turn until I thought we would stall out.

When the jungle rolled into view, he jerked the wings level and dropped the nose, pulling it back up a notch and boring down, down at the mountain. He aimed for the tree line at the base of the cliff. Suddenly the cannon burred, slicing ahead of us toward the cliff, and Shackler broke left. I didn't know if he hit any or not, but he yanked it around again for another pass.

"Buzz them," Shackler called, his voice tight in the turn. "Make 'em think you're strafing."

"Wilco," Wayne said.

"They'll catch on he's dry after the first pass," Shackler told me, "but it'll buy half a minute."

Wayne was pulling up as Shackler rolled again on target. He bore in closer, then let go with the cannon. I could see rocks chipping a hundred feet below the ledge. On the ledge the airman lay sprawled.

"Norm," Randy Wayne called. "I think he's dead."

"Looks that way."

Shackler brought it around again and sprayed till his cannon was dry. The body didn't move.

There was nothing to do but spiral up out of range and climb for altitude. Randy Wayne joined up on us in silent formation. Even as we climbed we could see soldiers from the mesa swarm to the ledge.

"Damn," Shackler said.

We kept climbing and as we reached twenty thousand another flight arrived, ready to descend.

"Duke Lead, this is Foxfire. What's the situation?"

"All dead," Shackler said crisply. "Blast it to hell."

"Roger, understand all friendlies are confirmed dead."

"That's affirmative," Shackler said. "We saw the only survivor die."

"Roger, Duke. Thanks for trying."

Shackler leveled off and eased back the throttle.

"Let's get these mothahs home," he said. "I'm nearly bingo on fuel."

After touchdown, Shackler taxied in and cut the engines and let the plane roll the last few feet to a stop on the ramp. I sat there not wanting to get out of the cockpit and have to write another *SNOW* report. I wondered why I had taken up history. Once through something like this was enough.

The ground crew ran with the wheel chocks and ladders and climbed up to help. Shackler lifted off his helmet and rubbed his gloved hands hard over his face.

"What the hell," he growled to his crew chief, waiting at the top of the ladder. "What the hell."

BIEN DIEN

Lebowitz stopped the jeep a mile short of the village. It was raining, a slow downpour which had already drenched us. A stream flowing out of the jungle rushed under a narrow bridge in front of us. Berrigan got out and I slid over by the door.

"Sure no one wants to come along?" Berrigan asked, drawing his fly rod from under the seat. He was a first lieutenant with a broad handsome face and sleepy eyes and a disdainful sneer. His job, like Croom's, had been phased out, and he passed the few days until his departure by fishing near Bien Dien. He was done with war and indifferent to Vietnam and seemed to care about nothing but rock music and trout fishing in streams he knew like a book up in Colorado.

"You catch 'em," Lebowitz said, racing the engine, "we'll eat 'em."

"Deal," Berrigan said, heading for the jungle. "See you here in a couple of hours."

The jeep lurched forward and rattled across the bridge and onto the road already turning to mud.

"Think we can make it?" Lebowitz asked over his shoulder. "Maybe we ought to go back." His face was drawn, his eyes deep-set in dark sockets, his stiff hair mostly white.

"I should get this stuff to the hospital," Hooker said grimly. "It might be the last shipment I'll get. You never can tell."

Hooker cushioned the box of medical supplies wrapped in a poncho on his lap like explosives. Croom sat easy beside him, his dark eyes narrowed at me, grinning. He was massive and handsome, his sinister eyes always the same, steady and masked under long hooded brows.

Lebowitz fought the wheel, his rain hood low over his eyes. "All right," he said, his high-pitched voice loud. "These jeeps go anywhere."

We bounced and slid along the road, the engine grinding, the rain and heat suffocating like a sweat box, and I found myself glancing from tree to tree, expecting sniper fire or even a python to drop down from an overhead branch. I'd been around Hooker long enough to know that your mind can play tricks on you.

It surprised me that Hooker was so determined to go on. Lebowitz had told me Hooker avoided the village for the last few weeks the way he hid from rockets. He came now only because Croom was along. It was pitiful, for he wasn't really needed there anymore. Everything big—the hospital, the schools, the orphanage—had been turned over to the Vietnamese.

Hooker had a broad, furrowed face. His right shoulder kept twitching and I must have been staring at it, for he shifted the box in his lap, glancing from me to the jungle, crow's feet wrinkling the edges of his eyes. He smoked constantly, one arm wrapped around the box, the fingers of his cigarette hand twitching.

Once he had been a good man, Lebowitz claimed. An ordained minister, a Little League coach, a counselor for ex-cons, a volunteer fireman. A chaplain who suffered the cold in Korea, decorated twice for valor. Later, he went to Brandeis for a Ph.D. in sociology, and lost his faith in Calvin. When his first wife died he left the church completely, went to Russia on a visa and lost his faith in sociology. Nowhere else to turn, he applied and was commissioned a captain in the line of the Air Force. Promoted to major ahead of his peers and after severe security screening was assigned to the Intelligence Corps in SAC Headquarters, Nebraska.

There, he started a scout troop in the ghetto, joined Big Brothers and after a year adopted a boy he sponsored. The kid knifed him in his sleep, took his wallet, a transistor, and the car and left him for dead. The car turned up wrecked in Colorado, and the boy was caught robbing a liquor store in Denver and sent to reform school.

When he recovered, Hooker was assigned to the nuclear plans section and began to go nuts when he saw what might actually happen. In 1962 during the Cuban missile crisis, Hooker worked night and day on the edge of doom, gathering evidence, putting it all into battle plans, foreseeing the last battle. If he had ever really lost it, in those nights he regained his faith in an angry God.

When Khrushchev pulled the missiles back to Russia, Hooker desperately took a month's leave and went back to Nebraska. He married a wealthy widow, an older woman who owned a castle in Maryland and who met Hooker years before at a Pentagon party, when he was a chaplain. After his marriage, Hooker flew to Maryland and back on weekends, nervous, gaining weight, until they eased him out of the nuclear plans section and then out of SAC altogether to an ROTC unit at a university. That was 1963, three months before President Kennedy was assassinated.

Now, a decade later, Hooker was still only a major. His wealthy wife died, leaving the mansion and a sizeable estate to him, but hopelessly tied up by suits brought by her children. Lonely, distraught, without a forgiving God, Hooker married a girl in the ROTC Angel Flight. I had seen her picture in an ornate frame in our room: a plain girl with glasses and buck teeth and huge tits bulging a sweater. Early, she ran up a debt against his expected settlement, still tied up in courts. She was unfaithful to him even before he was sent overseas last year, a volunteer for civic action.

They put him to work in the regional office at Bien Dien, a respectable job in charge of all the civic action projects in the central section of I Corps. But a month later all operations began phasing out because of troop withdrawals, except the unit at Bien Dien. Hooker brought all his old sociology books along in the engraved Morocco suitcase his new wife gave him, bought on credit. The textbooks by now were out of date. The leather mildewed rapidly in Bien Dien's humidity.

After his first rocket attack last summer, he stacked his books high on the floor, trying to raise his bed like a sanctuary. He slept under it every night, shell-shocked. The voice of doom was in every thunderclap of the monsoon, and he lived for months in paralyzing dread of the lightning bolt from Calvin's dark God with his name on it.

But after living with Croom for a while, Hooker left the relatively safe desk job and began risking fieldwork in nearby villages himself, as if determined to put himself in jeopardy in daylight, to submerge in the dangerous element and by the sheer power of the will to overcome.

Croom went with him whenever he could, pulling Hooker along toward an honorable DEROS with his own immunity. But although hundreds of people because of his building programs had roofs over their heads and clean well water to drink, he imagined sappers and land mines on every road and snipers in every tree, Asian shapes for a doom that haunted him all his life.

Ahead of us, the village looked deserted in the rain. From what Lebowitz had told me, I expected to see children everywhere, but the shacks were almost hidden in rain among trees and under the gray clouds that drifted by like battle smoke.

"Looks like no one's out today," I said, just to hear someone talk. Hardly anyone had said a thing since the rain began as we left the base. A new guy in Nam, I wanted to know what we might see, what the people thought of us, what the dangers were.

"Smarter than us," Croom called from the back. "Probably inside watching television."

"They have television here?" I asked, turning around, and saw Croom grinning at me.

Lebowitz laughed, slowing the jeep for a curve. "Gotta watch that cat," he said.

"Dumb bastards," I said, turning to the front again. "I don't think you know anymore than I do."

Croom laughed delightedly.

Lebowitz hit the brakes and I slammed into the dash.

"What is it?" Hooker cried, squeezing the box.

Lebowitz pointed. "Look."

There was something round impaled on a stake about four feet high, tilted between two trees not far from the first shack.

"Not another," Lebowitz said, shaking his head. He waited, the engine rolling heavily with a burned-out valve.

"Might as well drive on," Croom said.

"Don't you think we ought to see who it was?" Lebowitz asked.

Hooker clutched the box, drawing the poncho tighter over one side. His cheek twitched hard under one eye. "Look, can you turn around? We better go back for Berrigan."

"It's all right," Croom said.

"They do that kind of thing at night," Lebowitz said. "Probably sleeping it off, now." He put the jeep in neutral and got out. "We'd better take a look, don't you think, Croom?"

Croom swung himself over the side, but Hooker sat clutching the box. I got out and followed Lebowitz and Croom, who leaped the ditch filled with water. I could see what I thought was impaled on the stake, but I kept thinking surely it's not a human head.

But it was. Lebowitz got there first and leaned forward, hands on his knees, and Croom moved up beside him. I stood behind them and stared. It was already blackening on the stick like burned shish kabob, the rain streaking it like sauce. I felt stuff swarming up inside me and my lips pulled apart as if shriveling. The rain ran in my lips and I gagged.

Rain streamed down the matted hair and over the face and poured off the ragged flaps of meat that had been the neck. The jaw was distended, the lips puffed and stitched with thick cords like catgut. The head was thin, like a skull. One eye was jabbed out, and black matter had oozed down over the swollen cheek. The other eye stared, half-open.

"American?" Lebowitz asked, hands on his knees.

"Could be," Croom said.

Behind us the jeep rolled, idling.

"What have they done to the lips?" I asked, feeling my throat bulge up into my mouth.

"Balls," Lebowitz said. "They cut off the balls and stuff them in your mouth and sew them up like this." He shook his head.

Then he stood up, his lips pursed tight. "Want to take it down?"

Croom turned. "We'll get it on the way back."

I followed them to the jeep and leaped the ditch, almost sliding back into the rushing water.

"Who was it?" Hooker asked as we climbed into the jeep, which rolled sluggishly, puffing smoke.

"Nobody we know," Lebowitz said. He licked his lips and made a face, as if tasting buzzard guts. Years ago when he was an instructor pilot at Laredo, a buzzard crashed through his canopy, killing the student pilot in the front seat and splattering brains and buzzard guts all over Lebowitz. Nearly blinded, somehow he landed the plane, but he never flew with students again. Now he was the squadron's flying safety officer, careful, attentive to details, and the younger pilots called him Granny.

The jeep lurched ahead, and now I could feel them watching us from the trees. I steadied myself with one hand on the seat and wished Lebowitz would go faster, although we already bounced and sloshed so bad it seemed the wheels would break off.

We passed the first shack with its windows covered and rain pouring off the roof. We met no one on the narrow road that ran ahead for blocks into the rain, between fields and shacks and stands of jungle. At an intersection, Lebowitz turned left.

"Stop!" Hooker said.

Lebowitz hit the brakes and the jeep slid to a halt.

"What's wrong?"

Hooker clutched the box, his eyes darting from side to side down the road. "I don't know."

The engine bucked, sluggish, about to die. Lebowitz raced it.

"I've been down this road for months," Hooker said, his voice husky. "They're laying for me. I can feel it."

Dim in the clouds and pouring rain, the road ahead looked deserted, the shacks as far as we could see shut tight.

"It's probably just the rain," Lebowitz said, his hands trying to wipe the steering wheel dry.

"I don't know," Hooker said, and glanced at Croom. "I don't know."

"Back up," Croom said quietly. "We can go down past the church and come in behind the hospital."

"Is that all right?" Lebowitz called back.

Hooker kept pulling the poncho tight. "I don't know. Whatever Croom says."

Lebowitz ground the jeep into reverse and fought the steering wheel through the mud back to the main road. He lurched off between rows of shacks, in and out of the trees. They could have been anywhere in there, watching us.

At the Catholic Church, its bell tower almost hidden in clouds, Lebowitz slowed and bounced over a culvert and through two lanes of trees. Lebowitz reached down and switched on the headlights.

"Hurry!" Hooker screamed.

Lebowitz jammed the pedal and we raced through the shadows, and above the engine roar I thought I heard shots.

We sped out into the light, and up ahead in a wider clearing was the hospital, maybe a hundred people standing outside in the rain.

"Did you hear shooting?" Hooker asked, huddled over the box.

"Naw," Croom said, his arms folded. "Just echoes in the trees."

"What's everybody outside for?" Lebowitz asked, pulling up in front of the hospital, a long Air Force Quonset hut. He switched off the ignition. "Oh no," he said. "They've been hit again."

Three soldiers met us at the door. They looked like boys barely in their teens, but they carried rifles and wore ragtag camouflaged uniforms. They kept their rifles strapped on their shoulders, and they didn't move out of our way. One of them was on the first step and even then he barely came to Croom's chest.

Hooker put his knee up to get a better grip on the box and I took hold of one end. It was not all that heavy, but Hooker was trembling, breathing hard. Croom said something in Vietnamese and a soldier answered, wagging his head at us, his eyes narrowed.

There were families hunkered up against the building, some women weeping, children staring out at us with flat eyes.

The rain pebbled straight down. One of the boys opened the door and slipped inside and I caught flashes of white bandages inside, as if hundreds lay wounded. A Vietnamese in a doctor's robe, dark green splotched with blood, came out and stood in the doorway. A soldier hurried down and took the box from Hooker and me, and carried it quickly inside.

Croom wasn't arguing, just talking easy with the doctor in a tongue unavailable to me. Lebowitz turned toward the jeep and pulled my arm. He looked sick.

"Oh, God," he said.

I got into the jeep beside him and waited. Lebowitz kept licking his lips as if trying to get rid of a bad taste.

I tried to make out what Croom was saying. Croom turned to Hooker. He motioned, and Hooker stumbled forward as if in a daze. As Hooker went inside, Croom gave us a nod and followed him inside and the door closed.

Lebowitz put both hands on the steering wheel and hunched forward. Most of the people waited against the building, mourning. I settled back in the seat and rain poured off the poncho and down my face.

Lebowitz had his head down. His jaw muscles jerked and his fingers writhed on the steering wheel.

"Did you hear?" he asked.

"No."

"They say we hit the school this morning."

"Who?" I asked, feeling spiders crawl up my back.

"They say we did. Air-to-ground rocket. But it was a VC mortar. It had to be. I know that school. I used to come over with Hooker and play with the kids."

He looked up and pointed. "It's about a half mile from here, a hundred meters from ARVN military headquarters. The VC were probably aiming at that this morning and hit the school instead. Kids were out playing. Killed three, wounded fifteen. Two more aren't expected to live."

I could feel my head shaking back and forth. I looked at the families huddled in the rain.

"It might have been when Malatesta and I were up on the early scramble. We spotted a mortar site a few hundred meters north of here. Over that way. I remember aiming at the smoke where the FAC marked the mortar site. Damn, I hope we hit it! For the first time in my life I hope I killed someone."

His fist hit the wheel, the muscles of his jaw working. The soldiers at the hospital glared at us.

"They blaming us?"

"They can see I'm a pilot," he said, his hollow eyes staring ahead. "They don't know you. They know Hooker and Croom didn't do it."

He shook his head. "I used to come here with Hooker. There was this one beautiful little kid, eyes that would break your heart, about three years old. All her family had been killed by a mortar. Our flight surgeon landed by helicopter and worked on her most of the night. He must have put two hundred stitches in the kid. The whole squadron gave blood for her. I wrote my wife and we were going to adopt her."

"What happened?"

He shrugged. "They found a relative down near Saigon and one day a nun took her away. I guess she's down South, now. No one wanted me to have her, anyway."

He stopped, as if hearing something far off, going over something in his mind. "Naw," he said. "It couldn't have been a rocket. I knew what was in the village and I saw the mortar north of here and took careful aim. It couldn't have been."

I felt myself growing numb under the constant beating of rain. I shifted and water poured inside my hood. On the hospital steps, the soldiers stared at us, as if taking the measure of our heads.

Croom came slowly out of the building, his face showing nothing, his body like a giant's coming easily down the steps. Hooker followed him, an old man, his eyes blasted, his face twisted with grief. Croom helped him into the jeep, lifting him bodily into the seat. Croom went around to the other side and stepped in quietly and sat down.

Lebowitz sat there, staring ahead. Croom waited and then leaned forward.

"Hey, man," he said. "What's happening?"

Lebowitz shook his head, his jaws grinding. "That rocket," he said.

Croom glanced at me, his dark eyes masked, not showing

anything. "Yeah, it's too bad," he said easy, his teeth not moving, the line of his dark mustache even. "Probably a stray. That happens sometimes."

Lebowitz hit the steering wheel with both fists. "Damn it! It wasn't my rocket! It was a mortar, a VC mortar."

"Sure, man," Croom said, his eyes steady. "That's what it was."

"How do you know?" Lebowitz snapped. He turned in the seat and glared at Croom.

Croom merely shrugged.

"Maybe I did it," Lebowitz said. "Maybe one of my rockets strayed."

"When?"

"When I hit the mortar site!"

"No way," Croom said.

"It could have," Lebowitz said, the cords of his thin neck tight.

Croom sat there huge, his lips barely parted. "Easy, man," he said. "It's cool."

Lebowitz hit the switch and backed the jeep around, jerking, sloshing through the puddles into the narrow road.

Then, outside the village, Lebowitz stopped the jeep and Croom crossed the ditch and wrapped the head in a spare poncho. Croom pulled the stake out of the ground and smashed it against the nearest tree and came slowly back to the road.

Lebowitz got out and sat in the back beside Hooker, one hand covering his face.

Croom got in behind the wheel and drove slowly over the bridge, and on the other side, lying propped up against a tree, Berrigan waited. He saw us and held up a string of fish, a half dozen fine ones a pound or more each. While the jeep rocked from side to side, idling, like a boat in the rain, Berrigan stood up and gathered his fishing tackle. I made room on the seat and he settled in beside me.

He held up the catch again for us to see, a string of trout-like golden fat ones.

"Beauties," he said. "Took ten minutes. I've been asleep ever since."

Croom eased the jeep forward.

"Better make these your last," Lebowitz said, his voice tight.

"What do you mean?" Berrigan demanded.

Lebowitz kept a fist over his eyes. "Just don't go off alone anymore."

ROCKETS

Another mortar exploded a few hundred yards away.

Lebowitz was right. Mortars did not crack sharply like rockets, but impacted more like a watermelon or a body bursting on pavement. I lay still and watched for lights.

"Croom?" I heard Lebowitz whisper.

Mortars again, three or four in a row.

"Moose?" Lebowitz said aloud.

"Yeah?" I answered.

"Better get your pants on."

I was lying with them on. I got up as quietly as I could and got my wallet and keys from the dresser. Weird behavior. Somehow it seemed best not to panic.

The siren began winding up.

"Where's Croom?" I asked.

He scooped change from the chest and dropped it in a pocket. "Out walking around."

"Again?" I asked, not wanting to believe.

"I told you, he's crazy. Gone to the perimeter, as always. Don't worry, they can't kill him."

Over thirty, Lebowitz was the only pilot of my three roommates. Married, he was the squadron's flying safety officer, meticulous, dedicated to saving lives. He had a thin high-keyed voice that didn't fit his apparent calm. His face always looked drawn, almost emaciated, his eyes deep-set in dark hollow sockets, his stiff hair pepper white.

Lebowitz bent down. "Hooker, come on," he said. He was on one knee, calling under the bunk. "Those were mortars. They're more accurate than rockets."

"No," Hooker said, his voice muffled by a pillow.

72

"You'd better come on," Lebowitz coaxed.

In the dark I saw movement, as if he were trying to pull Hooker out from under the bed.

"Leave me alone!" Hooker said, his voice deeper in the pillow.

The siren wailed and farther off more mortars hit. My feet felt the concussions.

"Go on, Moose," Lebowitz said. "I'll stay with him."

I hesitated. "Can I help?"

Two rockets crashed down nearby. I dropped to the floor. Terrible, like the end of the world, like close thunder and a screen door slamming.

Someone shouted outside on the stairs.

I stood up breathing hard, trembling, ready to go.

"Come on, Hooker," Lebowitz said, straining. Then, "Give me a hand, Moose."

I helped drag Hooker out. Hooker grabbed the bed and it crashed down off the stacks of books. Lebowitz tore Hooker's fingers away from the bed rail, and I grabbed the flak vest Hooker always wore at night and pulled him out to the middle of the room. He was moaning.

"Lift him up," Lebowitz said.

We dragged him between us through the door. He was heavy, limp, and the stairs seemed to go down, down forever. The siren wailed louder than I had ever heard it. Another rocket hit a few hundred yards away and I almost dropped him.

We reached the bunker and dragged him to the middle. It was dark but I could see someone shifting out of the way. We put him down between us and he leaned against the wall.

"Is he hurt?" someone asked.

"Tired," Lebowitz said. "He hasn't been able to sleep."

"Hell, me neither," someone said.

"The bastards are getting serious," another added.

Someone laughed, too loud.

On a radio there was music playing, something from the forties that seemed completely out of place.

"Phil," Hooker moaned to Lebowitz.

"Easy," Lebowitz said, "easy." He grabbed Hooker's shoulders and held him.

Lebowitz had told me it was coming, if they didn't ship Hooker home. Hooker was still only a major, the last civic action officer on the base. Now that every big project—the hospital, the schools,the orphanage—had been turned over to the Vietnamese, ready for the American pullout, Hooker was superfluous, nothing more in his own mind than a sitting target.

"God, God," Hooker groaned.

A rocket hit a half mile away and suddenly the whole world seemed to explode. The bunker shook and dust fell and I thought, earthquake. A new deep booming, again and again, like rolling thunder.

"They've hit the bomb storage!" someone said.

The overhead timbers shook and dust streamed down. A series of bombs exploded almost at once, and clumps of dust fell on us. Hooker spasmed against me and I grabbed his head to keep him from beating it on the wall.

"Easy!" Lebowitz shouted between explosions.

I could feel the vibrations in the bench before I heard the jet roar. Then the crackling boomed louder and I held Hooker's head. It sounded like the whole squadron of F-4s taking off.

Hooker stood up and shuffled away, moaning, then broke for the tunnel. A man across from me slammed into him and another grabbed his shoulders and they wrestled him to the bench. Lebowitz helped them hold him down. He struggled a moment, then fell back, coughing.

"No sweat," one of them said.

I heard Hooker retch and splatter in the dirt. He heaved and moaned, heaved and fell back against the wall.

"If he can't take it, send the bastard home."

"Shut up, Malatesta," Lebowitz said.

The voice rang out of nowhere, resonant, almost cheerful. "Nice place you have here."

"Croom," Lebowitz called, his voice strained. "We need you."

Croom stretched his hands against the beams of the entrance. Then he dropped them and bent forward into the tunnel.

A voice on the radio relayed a call for the disaster control team, second shift, and two men slipped out of the bunker.

"Keep down, keep down!" the radio announcer kept shouting. He forgot to cut out the music and it sliced through everything with bizarre frivolity. "They're aiming at the U.S. sector! Stay in your bunkers, this is a red alert!"

"Cut that off!" someone ordered, and the radio went dead. "It's that kid, Fleming. That bastard's in trouble. I'm going to have his ass canned tomorrow."

I didn't need much to push the panic button myself. I wondered how Colonel Tydings expected me to write anything worthwhile about this. A few old hands like Lebowitz could say it better. Now, bombs kept exploding, and mortars. For a while only the wailing siren, then an explosion like an earthquake's aftershock.

"Remember the artillery dump they hit at Da Nang?" Croom asked, tall in the tunnel. "Shells kept going off for a year. Night and day. You never knew if it was an attack or not."

"Where have you been?" someone taunted Croom, breaking the tension. "You and Lieutenant Hassan been to the perimeter again?"

"Oh, sweet Hannah Hassan!" someone moaned. "I'd go to the perimeter if Hassan was along to nurse me."

"I'd go anywhere with Hannah Hassan," another said. "Anywhere, anytime."

Croom laughed, a low rumble, as if he was enjoying this.

"Croom," Lebowitz said again. "We need you here, man."

Then Croom must have seen Hooker, for he took the distance in three or four steps, bent down and lifted Hooker like a rag doll and straightened him up on the bench.

"Hey, man," he said in Hooker's direction. "How they hanging?"

Hooker said nothing, just slumped against the wall and put one hand to his face.

Croom beckoned for us with his head and I leaned nearer. "When did he break?" Croom asked.

"After the rockets," Lebowitz whispered. "Hell, I'm sorry. I couldn't seem to help him."

"Easy," Croom told him. "You did fine."

Croom settled back against the wall and I heard him slap Hooker's knee.

Hours, but maybe only five minutes later, the siren stopped. Men soon began leaving the bunker. Another bomb exploded and two men ran back inside and stood laughing at themselves in the tunnel.

"Hey, man," one said. "It all counts toward DEROS."

The two disappeared again, leaving only three or four shapes along the walls. Hooker was shaking all over, his body palsied. We released him and he slumped on the bench, trembling, his tongue clicking dry when he opened his mouth, whispering to himself.

Croom spoke quietly. "Hey, man, want to go see Hannah?"

Except for his tongue clicking like glue, Hooker was quiet, shaking violently.

"Run upstairs and get his keys," Lebowitz told me. "We'll take the jeep."

The hospital was a series of connected barracks, a single bulb burning over each entrance. I parked the jeep where Lebowitz pointed and hurried around to help lead Hooker to the building.

Hooker shuffled along between us, his arms trembling. Down the road an ambulance truck was off-loading at another ward. Corpsmen hurried with stretchers and the truck doors slammed and it roared away.

A helicopter with a flashing red light settled out of the dark sky toward a lighted helipad across the road. Three corpsmen waited to meet it.

Croom knocked softly on the locked door, knocked again, and soon the door opened. A young corpsman in fatigues stood in the doorway. He saw Hooker and stepped aside for us to enter.

"Is Lieutenant Hassan on duty?" Croom asked quietly, leading Hooker.

"Yes, sir, she's here," the corpsman said.

"Could the major see her?"

The corpsman studied Hooker and stepped back. "This way," he said, and led us down the dim aisle between rows of beds to the nurses' station at the center of the long ward. The ward was packed with beds jammed close together.

Croom led him to the desk and stood by her, where she sat sleeping in a lounge chair in a circle of light. Croom leaned down and whispered to Hannah, and when she looked up and saw him she smiled.

Hannah Hassan leaned forward under the lamp, her dark hair soft above her white uniform. I caught only a glimpse of her face before she left the light and rose to meet us, but she was stunning. So help me, Croom, I thought to myself, I won't lay a hand on her, but I love her.

"He's tired, Hannah," Lebowitz said, his eyes in the lamp's glow hollow as a skull. "He's just tired."

She reached out for Hooker's arm, her breasts swelling the starched uniform.

Above the lamp she was lovely, wide eyes and full lips and a revealing neckline. Her hair lay in loose swirls close to her eyes, curling out beyond her eyes, almost like a veil. She made me think of oases and camels laden with fruit, fig trees and wineskins beaded with moisture, thick scented cushions and tents and long hot nights. She wore heavy golden half-moon earrings, erotically unmilitary.

Lebowitz asked her, "Can you give him something to let him sleep?"

Hannah nodded and her dark eyes shimmered. She turned to me and smiled, so slightly.

"Hannah," Croom said, "the Little Moose. Our new roommate. He's here to do a *SNOW* job, but don't hold that against him." She nodded slowly and gave me that look again.

"Would you like to sit here with me?" she asked Hooker, her voice low.

She pulled his arm and Hooker slumped next to her into a chair. He kept plowing his fingers through his gray hair, his hand jerking.

"If," Hooker said, his eyes finding hers, trying to explain, "if a rocket hits . . . just like that," and he tried to snap his fingers. "Don't you see?"

Croom pushed her chair closer and Hannah took Hooker's hand in both of hers.

"Bring Dr. Sanders," Hannah said softly to a corpsman.

If. Speculation could drive anyone mad. I had listened to Hooker rave about a doom he couldn't escape. Poor bastard. Fire and brimstone weren't just a metaphor to him. Years ago as an ordained chaplain, he developed doubt and frostbite in Korea and traded his cross for a Regular Air Force commission. In the early sixties, on the staff of the Strategic Air Command's nuclear plans office, he caught a glimpse at the horrors of Armageddon and regained his faith in an avenging God.

"I know what's going to happen," Hooker told us a few nights before, a cigarette between his twitching fingers. "I've seen the bombs, the ICBMs." He shook his head. "Unspeakable firepower. Think about all we've got, the things that could go wrong. It's more than a man can take, Phil."

Hooker had turned to me, his eyes old and dark. He sucked deep on the cigarette and let the smoke trickle out. "You think you can take it, don't you, Mosely? Listen," he said, the cigarette trembling between his fingers. "You think a 122 rocket is bad? It's not bad. Wait till you're cleared Top Secret. You'll see things you've never dreamed of. You ever have nightmares, Mosely? Bad ones?"

I shrugged. "Sure. Bad enough."

Hooker broke into a fit of coughing, then fell back, staring at me, and lit another cigarette. "That's nothing," he had warned, his face red. "You wait."

Like Pip abandoned in the ocean by shipmates chasing a whale, Hooker saw God's doom in random explosions, and for this, we called him mad. There seemed only two ways to go—crazy with worry, or like Croom, somehow turn it off. Watching Hooker slumped in the mental ward, I wanted to try it Croom's way, not think about it, just breathe and go home.

Another bomb exploded now, and Hooker jerked against the desk. Lebowitz grabbed for him and Hannah put her hands on Hooker's knees. Lebowitz lit a cigarette and put it between his lips. Hooker took a drag and kept staring at the floor.

Hannah moved to the edge of her chair, her white dress inches above her knees, her wonderful legs close together. She took Hooker's wrist and held it on her knees, found his pulse and began stroking his wrist with her little finger.

She touched a watch over her left breast and looked down to time his pulse. Her brows arched wide and her lashes, dark and long, never seemed to flicker.

The way she kept moving that finger on Hooker's wrist was driving me mad. I looked at her neck shimmering smoothly like a dancer's. I saw Croom grinning at me from above the light, his face dark and massive, his teeth even and white. Big bastard. Grinning, he winked at me.

The corpsman came back with the doctor, an older psychiatrist with glasses who waited with his hand on Hooker's shoulder while Hannah briefed him.

"A hundred milligrams of Thorazine," the doctor said in a quiet voice, and the corpsman went to the medicine case behind Hannah and unlocked the door. He brought a pill and a paper cup of water to Hooker.

"Let's go," Croom said.

Lebowitz glanced at Hannah, and she nodded.

"We're admitting the major," the doctor said. He turned to the corpsman. "Put him in a bed near the nurses' station and schedule him with me after he wakes up this morning."

Croom held up a hand for us to wait, walked back and bent close to Hooker's ear. The corpsman started to remove Hooker's flak vest, but Hooker clutched it and leaned back. Hannah shook her head at the corpsman.

Croom stopped by Hannah's chair and squeezed her neck. She reached for his hand and kissed it, then he came back and led us outside. "He'll be all right," he said.

Back outside in the night, we found another ambulance truck at the surgical ward, red light whirling. Flames shot up from three fires we could see. The damp air reeked like sulphur, a breeze blowing down from the bomb dump. The night was wild with trucks and helicopters and now and then the rapid fire of M-16s.

"Sappers?" I asked, wondering if they would storm the base tonight.

Croom listened. "Naw, nothing to worry about."

He looked up at the sky. "Just kids firing at shadows," he said, and I wondered how I could ever learn enough about war to stay alive.

≡TURNING ON≡

The voice rang out of nowhere, resonant, almost cheerful. "You cats having fun in there?"

"Croom!" Lebowitz called, his voice shrill. "Get in here before they blow your head off."

Croom entered the bunker and stood massive in the shaft of moonlight. It was a crazy feeling, something that happened every night and might go on forever. This was the second rocket attack, the second time in two hours we had been to the bunker.

Someone flicked a cigarette lighter, and it lit up like a torch in the bunker.

Croom laughed and shook his head. Slowly, looming in the flame's wavering shadows, he raised his arms and pressed against both sides of the tunnel.

"Nice place you have here," he said. He looked slowly at each of us, testing the walls. "Did I ever tell you guys about Tet a few years ago? This cat and I were waiting in base ops for a flight up to Da Nang. They threw hundreds of those 122s in night after night. We had this big plate glass window looking out on the flight line, see. I was flaked out on the floor, trying to sleep, and this cat's pacing up and down by that window as if it's a mirror. A 122 slammed down not fifty feet away. That glass stripped him down to the bone like machetes."

No one said anything. I looked up at the beamed ceiling supporting the layers of sandbags. The siren wailed.

"Lebowitz," Croom said. "Let's go for a walk."

"No way," Lebowitz said. "I'm sleeping here. I've got to see those films in the morning."

He was still worried about that rocket attack on the school. His target films would be ready hours from now. I dreaded to know what he might find, that his own stray rocket might have hit it.

"How about you, Moose?" Croom called, grinning wide. "You could do a *SNOW* report on perimeters."

Croom stood easy in the harsh shaft of moonlight. His dark wide-set eyes were deep under long hooded brows.

I didn't want to go. It was crazy to risk the perimeter of the base at night, and I was still shaky from tonight's rockets. But I didn't want to end up on a mental ward like Hooker, either. So I said okay, and then as we left the bunker and entered the dark, I wondered if I would end up crazy like Croom.

Outside, an ambulance truck roared by, red light whirling. The damp breeze blew sulphur and smoke down from the bomb dump, hit by a rocket a few hours ago. The base was a chaos of a wailing siren and vehicles driven by men trying to survive an attack they couldn't see.

Croom walked easy, that big slow stride of his, each foot sure of itself before landing. He was like a bat, but I had to stare to stay with him. After a mile the sounds of trucks on the base died away and the M-16 bursts faded, and when we had walked a while longer it was as if the flight line had shut down. We passed clumps of trees like dark holes, darker than night. Anything could have been in there. It was crazy.

I began hearing things behind us but didn't turn and look because I might lose track of Croom. The hair on my neck rose and my fists ached like before a wrestling match. I shook them loose. I couldn't see ten feet in front of me, and easy as I could walk, all I could hear were my own footsteps.

It dawned on me that Croom had gone back, had left me out here as a joke. Take the new guy on a snipe hunt. I walked faster, almost a trot, and bumped into something low like a stump.

"Easy," Croom said, behind me. I had passed him. "We're almost to the wire."

I fell back beside him, feeling foolish. "How can you tell?" I asked, my voice a whisper.

"Velocity," he said. "So far in so much time. The ground, too. Feel it with your toe. Wood chips, where they cut the trees, like a firebreak. The perimeter wire runs through here, unless they've cut it again."

He touched my arm and we veered left along the wire, and soon he stopped and pulled me down, back to back with him. I listened hard to hear if we had been followed. Nothing. From sheer fatigue, I began to relax. I could hear explosions in the distance, like thunder, not that far away.

Later, the overcast broke and stars came out, giving a vague outline to the trees. I turned my head and could see Croom. A bomb went off in the dump and I flinched, thinking at first it was a rocket. Mosquitoes whirred around my neck, but caution told me not to slap them. Too loud. I remembered I hadn't taken malaria pills for weeks since I left Saigon. The least of my worries, now. I thought I heard something across the wire, but Croom didn't move. After listening for minutes, I gave up and relaxed again against his back, broad and firm as the dark.

I couldn't figure why Croom stayed in Nam, for he was on his third tour. He'd been an Air Commando, Lebowitz had said. They inserted him by boat into the North or dropped him in by helicopter and he lived off the land for weeks, sometimes months at a time. He was always grinning. Crazy. Had to be to survive what he had gone through. Assassinations, Lebowitz said, and sabotage of targets the F-4s weren't allowed to hit from the air. Christ only knows what all.

He was out for months, then one day he'd show up at Da Nang or Pleiku or here at Bien Dien and someone would recognize him in the officers' club. He'd be thin and mean-looking and they'd say, "How they hanging, Croom?" And he'd say, "They hanging fine," and sit there sipping coffee and kind of grinning to himself.

I realized I wasn't sweating, the first time since leaving Saigon. The breeze was muggy but cooler than among the buildings, and the air was clean without jet fuel and human waste, and slightly sweet, like harvest. Stars kept breaking out from clouds until the sky was a bowl of familiar constellations.

I felt it pierce and smeared it with my palm, feeling the blood spread on my neck. You didn't have to slap them, I was learning. I wondered how long it took Croom to learn how to survive his missions alone. It must be something you never want to lose. Maybe that's why he kept coming out at night, keeping the instincts sharp. For what other cause, I wondered.

"It's nice, here," I said, low as I could.

"Shhh," he said. "Told you you'd like it."

I imagined him grinning. I wondered, though, if he bothered to grin in the dark.

"How long do you stay?"

I felt him shrug. "Till the rockets start. Or till I feel like it."

"Why the rockets?"

He shrugged again. "They won't come around after the rockets start."

"They?"

"VC."

I wondered if that was something moving beyond the wire. "You mean they're out here tonight?"

"Maybe. Probably not. They used to come by every night or so. They waited for me, until I learned all the good hiding places. Then I waited for them and they stopped coming. All the old cats, that is."

"You killed them, here?"

He shrugged.

"They know you keep coming?"

"Word gets around. Now and then some kid tries it, or some superstar down from the North who wants to make a local name for himself."

He turned his head, and I knew he was grinning. "Don't panic," he said. "They don't come here much anymore. This is my country, man."

My country? It was Mars, another galaxy, the trees between us and the base so tall, the night so absolute, there was not even a glow from the buildings. Unless another bomb exploded, I wouldn't know which way to return. It was rich country, the ground fertile with ages of decay. I lifted a handful of loam, the moist dirt easy to pack like clay. I held it under my nose and broke it, the odor warm and heady like my uncle's greenhouse.

"What did you do before you joined up, Croom?"

"Nothing."

I shook my head. "You could do anything."

I think he laughed. "Sure, man. Pump gas, pimp, play bad-dude-on-the-block."

I felt something creeping up on us, but Croom did nothing, so I kept quiet. I tried to look around at Croom's country, but all I could see were the stars.

He moved away to relieve himself, and so did I. We sat down again, but facing the opposite way. I couldn't see any difference. As the night wore on, he told about his first year as an enlisted man in the Air Force, a flunky in the motor pool on a base in Georgia. Then a brother from New York told him about the Air Commandos, and soon he was in and out of training and deep in the jungles of South America. He wouldn't say which country. He had a year in Laos in '65, even before I heard of the place. I was in school, then, winning a wrestling scholarship to Ball State.

In Laos he stepped on a mine that smashed his leg and broke his back. That was when he learned to walk easy, he said. He lay in traction for months and thought about what he had seen in Laos and decided the hell with it. They offered him a medical discharge and he turned it down and just left, his enlistment over. Back home he started college on the GI Bill, drank and fought too much and flunked out. In Canada he played football for half a season until his leg hobbled him so much he couldn't get out of a three-point stance. He wintered in the Florida Everglades as a guide and by spring the leg had healed.

He started back to training camp but missed the flight and said the hell with it and flew up to Washington instead. On a whim he called his old commander from Laos, the captain who had put him in for the Silver Star. After an evening of drinking, the captain talked him into a series of applications and officer qualification tests, on which Croom scored outstanding. Now, he took sarcastic delight in saying it: *outstanding*.

With those scores and his service record, especially the Silver Star, he got an appointment to Officer Training School. What the hell, he thought, and three months later was a lieutenant on his way to his old outfit. After that, he spent most of his life in the jungles, South America again and Laos, but most of the time, Vietnam.

He said all this with his back to me and in a voice so low I wasn't sure at times if I really heard him or only made it up. I thought of my Thursday afternoons in ROTC drill and wrestling matches and graduate school in the library and the march on Washington. Man, I had really lived.

Colonel Tydings knew better than to expect me to write anything worthwhile, at least at first. Maybe he just wanted me to get my feet wet. The hours I had spent digging through old reports, all the cassettes I had filled so far were just priming. Later, if I survived, maybe I'd learn what to write.

I wondered if I would find the big picture in the *SNOW* reports, or if most of them were written by outsiders like me. As Croom told me my first week here, everyone's an expert. I thought of the fable of the blind men's first impressions of an elephant. The one who touched the tail went home and said an elephant is like a rope; the one who touched the leg said it was a tree trunk. I'll bet the poor fool who stood under the elephant's ass at the wrong time went back and said he'd been to Vietnam.

Who could put all the pieces together? Could anyone make any sense of a war? Colonel Tydings? A ground-pounder, like me. Lebowitz? Could even Croom?

Maybe. But what kind of crazy sense was this, waiting?

I thought of the rockets and mortars tonight, and the jets roaring on takeoff. Yes, there was a kind of glory in war, living desperately on the edge, like Croom here in the dark in his country. That was what turned Sheila and me and maybe thousands of others on in those holy days of protest. We were crusaders, baring our souls to the bayonets, feeling beaten down but unvanquished, part of a righteous cause.

Now I saw that in a war, where anything can happen, some could be turned on more by danger than they could ever be again, the way some lovers bind each other, thrilled by the sensual helpless risk.

Out here, Croom knew the risks. He lived in a Manichean world, but at least out here he knew where he stood. Everything that moved spoke with a knife, and Croom knew the language—the basic Esperanto, the terms of survival. Here there was no question of why. Only how.

The big beast. He was six-eight and two-hundred-fifty and the bravest man I ever met. Everywhere he went, walking slow and lean and wearing that perfect polished steel mask, he carried in his flesh a poised indifference to death. Sitting back to back with him, now, I felt what the hell, you only die once. But the mask forming on my face felt more like a protective sneer than a grin.

A rocket crashed down on the base. Even though I saw the flash, I flinched when the concussion reached us. Croom only turned his head.

"Third time tonight," was all he said.

A barrage of seven or eight rockets hit almost at once, crashing randomly around the base, fierce, loud, even out here. It must be horrible to be hit by one, wounded but not killed, shell shocked, almost destroyed. No wonder Ahab went mad, haunted by the jaws of Moby Dick. You might go on hearing it explode the rest of your life, waiting for it before sleep, replaying it in dreams that would never be safe again.

But out here with Croom backing me up, for the first time I felt like an observer. So this was how he looked on us every night, cringing in our bunker as if tons of sand could save us from high explosives. The sky yawned black over the base, the vast universe pierced with meteors on random trajectories, points in times which finally, in the total scheme, made no difference at all.

Somehow, Croom was able to turn it off. For the time I wanted to try it his way, just keep my eyes open and watch it happen.

"Ready?" he said.

"You call it," I answered.

He stood up and I followed him, glad to find my legs rested. I believed he was taking another way back. I don't know how, but it felt that way. Exciting, learning to do, not having to worry why.

We walked until we could hear jet roar and choppers and the thin wail of the base siren, and suddenly we could see the lights of the base. Another rocket crashed with a bright flash, and flames raged high along the horizon.

"What's that?"

"Must have hit the fuel storage," Croom said. "Acres and acres of big rubber bladders full of jet fuel."

"How will they stop it?"

"Fight it," he said. "It could blow up in their faces, though."

What a strange feeling, striding along with him in the dark toward the flames, like the first big match I won in high school, so pumped up I wanted to take on the champ.

"Think we should go help?" I asked.

Under the orange glow I could see his face, even his features. He turned and grinned down at me.

"A little bearcat, aren't you? Told you this would be good for you."

"What the hell," I said, trying to wipe the smirk away.

We walked on in silence. Two more rockets hit before we reached the first buildings.

"Kerosene burns too hot," he said. "We couldn't get close enough without asbestos suits. Let's get some sleep."

As we made our way through the base to our barracks, I caught glimpses of the fire burning wildly. It turned everything orange and I had to smile at Croom strolling easily along, looking like the devil at home, easy as hell. And me with him, the sorcerer's apprentice. A month at Bien Dien and strutting as if I were Croom. Too much.

I climbed the stairs behind him, the siren rising and falling, the bunker behind us dark and probably packed. I wanted to ask if we should bunker down, but I couldn't stand for Croom to laugh at me. Not after tonight.

Croom sat on his bed and pushed off his shoes and lay down slowly and without speaking turned his face to the wall. I think he was asleep even before I lay back on my bunk, hands under my head, watching the orange shadows lick the ceiling like flames, about to catch fire.

LEBOWITZ

Lebowitz skipped breakfast and hurried to the film lab before his mission. At the flight line mess, Croom and I heard that the morning briefings had been cancelled. Rumors flew everywhere. Someone said the NVA divisions north of us had captured two more camps. He claimed the mortars and rockets last night killed dozens of Vietnamese, but someone else said hundreds. Someone said the VC overran half of Bien Dien village and slaughtered scores of villagers during the night.

We were about to leave when Lebowitz came to the mess hall and stood in the doorway like a ghost. I nudged Croom.

Croom carefully put down his coffee and shoved back. "Let's go," he said. "That cat's got troubles."

His deep eyes were red as if he had been crying. Croom took him by the arm and led him outside into the bright light. Lebowitz put his hand over his eyes and stumbled along. Two sergeants saluted and held their salutes as they passed by and stared sideways at us.

"Hey, man," Croom said quietly. "What's happening?"

Lebowitz kept his hand over his eyes. I thought no, not to Lebowitz. Not that.

"Easy," Croom said to him. "How do you know?"

"The films," Lebowitz said through gritted teeth.

Croom shrugged. "Hey, what can they show?"

"Come see for yourself," he snapped.

At the film lab an airman took us into a viewing room like a long broom closet. He cut out the lights and the projector shot an image to the front screen.

"Now, watch," Lebowitz said bitterly behind us. "See? The FAC put his smoke there, close to the village."

90

I saw the shadow of the Forward Air Controller's OV-10 banking away from the zone he had marked.

"Okay, look, we're lined up on target. Malatesta blipped us right about *there*. Watch. See that? See it? Oh, God! Look at it, look at it go."

And that was all. The screen went white, the end of the film click-clicking behind us. The projector cut off and we sat there in the dark.

"You see?" Lebowitz snapped.

Croom probably shrugged. "I saw a lot of smoke."

"Look, you saw it. One of my own rockets killed those kids!"

"It might have been a mortar," Croom said quietly as the lights clicked on.

"Naw, naw," Lebowitz said, his lips pulled back. "You saw the FAC's smoke several hundred meters north of the buildings. You saw me roll in and Malatesta lock us. The pod zipped down ahead and clustered around the smoke. I got the mortar position, I surely got it. But you saw it—one rocket ran away the moment I fired. It zipped up out of sight, high and to the left. They do that sometimes. As I started the pull-out you saw a flash come on the film. It hit the school yard. You saw the angle. It was my stray rocket."

"Maybe," Croom said.

"It was!" Lebowitz shouted. "I ran it back and forth a dozen times. You think I want to believe this? The angle's there, the timing fits. It was mine."

"Ready?" Lebowitz yelled behind him. "Roll it again!"

The film flared on the screen and we watched it winding before the bulb. First came the FAC's marking smoke, then the roll-in, and the smoke in the jungle looming nearer, nearer. And the flash of rockets and sure enough, like a comet hurtling wildly out of its orbit, one of the rockets smoked high and to the left. And then the pullout, sudden, six or seven Gs. I felt myself tightening not to black out.

The target dropped out of the picture and the buildings

slid down in its place and there was a sudden flash off to the left in the school yard. The film was not sharp, not in good focus, and the blurry little specks, like amoebae under a microscope, suddenly around the edges of the flash looked like bodies hurling through space. Then the horizon cut the film like a terrible whiteness at the end.

Croom was silent, even after the clicking of the film ceased. I felt the taste of steel and acid in my throat as if I had swallowed a sword.

"You gotta shake it off, man," Croom said at last.

Lebowitz let out a cry.

"Come on," Croom said, standing up. "We'll go wake Hannah."

Lebowitz jerked his arm away.

Croom kept his grin. "Naw, man. You got to shake it off."

Croom led him outside and Lebowitz raised his hand to his eyes. "Come on, man," Croom said, his teeth showing. "Let's go see Hannah."

I watched them turn toward the nurses' hootch. Lebowitz stumbled away with his hand to his eyes like some blind Oedipus, with Croom striding slowly behind.

The morning was already hot. I felt sweat pooling inside my flight cap. There were Phantoms taking off again, thundering like the end of the world. For somebody today out there in the jungle, it would be. Poor Lebowitz, I thought. Poor bastard.

I was still fumbling with the oxygen connector as our F-4 hurtled down the runway. Without Lebowitz to check on me, I wasn't sure I was hooked up right. I could see myself at twenty thousand feet passing out with Shackler humming "Okie from Muskogee" and looking around for someone to bomb.

But like a roller coaster, the F-4 leaped into the air, committed. I was breathing, and my lap belt felt tight. The survival vest and partial G-suit clutched me, so I folded my hands and thought what the hell.

Randy Wayne was on our wing again, smooth, in close, close enough for me to read Wayne on his helmet, and on his canopy rail, in red script bordered in black, 688th. Three red stars for MiGs he had shot down were painted underneath. He had already flown the dawn mission but was up again in place of Lebowitz. His two-hundred-ninety-fourth mission.

Shackler jerked hard left and kept climbing. Randy never flared a foot either way, in tight formation, but somehow his turn seemed smoother. I hoped I could fly with him someday.

Behind him in the rear seat Malatesta hunched forward, squat, his turtle-shell head barely showing above the canopy rail. "Serves the cocksucker right," Malatesta had scoffed when I told them what Lebowitz thought he had done. "I warned him he was in too close."

Dumb bastard.

Humming something country, Shackler leveled off at twenty-two thousand and yanked the throttles back, loitering in the northwest quadrant.

"What's the mission?" I asked.

"Hummm?"

"What's the mission today?"

Humming. Finally, Shackler said, "Relax. Something will turn up. A FAC'll find us a target."

I looked around but couldn't see a Forward Air Controller or any other aircraft anywhere. The sky was clear and deep and, for the time being, even the radio was quiet. Low in the west toward Laos there was a buildup of thunderheads, but nothing that could reach us for hours. My oxygen mask was tight and I was breathing fine. No sweat.

"What about Bu Cai?" I asked.

"Hum?"

"The Special Forces camp. Is it safe today?"

"Nothing's safe." Humming. "Don't sweat it. Something will break."

Before I could settle back, a voice called in, "Target."

I saw Shackler glance to the right at Randy Wayne as we listened to the FAC's target report.

"Roger, Fat Cat," Shackler answered, already rolling into a turn west. "This is Duke Flight Leader with two Phantoms on the way from your six o'clock position, two-two thousand. Clear us in wet, three minutes from now, over."

"Roger, Duke Lead," the FAC answered. "Watch for my smoke along the old Ranchhand trail. Activity was in the trees just west of the trail, likely part of a convoy stopped for the day. I must have caught some dude out sunning himself."

Shackler steepened the dive, and a few miles away I could see the dead swathe through the jungle.

"Fat Cat," Shackler radioed. "Confirm this is a free-fire zone."

"That's affirmative," the FAC answered immediately. "Burn anything that moves. Are you carrying low-drag ordinance?"

"My number two has low-drag bombs. Right, Randy?"

"Affirm," Randy Wayne replied.

The FAC continued, "Then I'll set some smoke just inside the trees. If there's a convoy, that's where it'll be."

"Roger."

Shackler hummed, his head pivoting around the cockpit from one switch to another, setting up for the run. I glanced around at my own maze of dials and devices and felt stupid.

Down ahead, the jungle loomed rapidly up at us. Still ignorant of aerodynamics, I felt my feet plant themselves on the floor, and my neck stiffened. Shackler seemed to have his head in the cockpit and I started to ask if it was time to pull out when he radioed, "Fat Cat, I see your smoke. I have you at my ten o'clock position. Coming through ten thousand. Am I cleared?"

"Roger, Duke Leader, cleared in wet. Aim about two hundred meters south of my smoke."

"Randy," Shackler called, "spread out and behind. I'll spray the edge and you drop yours just south of the smoke."

"Roger."

Randy Wayne broke behind us as Shackler dumped our nose even steeper, the plane buffeting like dive brakes. Then he yanked on the stick and we began mushing out, mushing, and I thought God, we're going to hit.

But the jungle began to blur by underneath, the trail we zoomed above deserted, the trees along it dead and brown as if a controlled forest fire had wiped out a swathe two hundred meters on each side. A Ranchhand trail, sprayed by Agent Orange in C-123s five or ten years ago.

We swooped along near the speed of sound, barely a hundred feet above the trees. It was like skimming history in a time machine. One of my ROTC instructors had been in Ranchhands in '66. He showed us 8-millimeter films of his operations over jungle like this, but green unbroken, no hint of trails spinning through all that foliage. And now here it was, or here I was skimming along over a trail, and there was nothing alive to see.

Then the FAC's smoke drifted up like a campfire and Shackler fired the cannon near it, a loud burring as shells like a laser beam drilled the edge of the trail. The Phantom shuddered as if a cable tugged at it from behind, and I felt Shackler tap the rudder to spray the smoke with cannon fire, before it flashed by underneath. He jerked into a climb and I saw sweat drops splatter against the inside of my sun visor. When he leveled out, sunlight burst on the visor like blood.

I looked back too late to see Randy Wayne's pass. His explosions seemed little more than smoke, filtered and absorbed by the dense trees. No wonder they started Ranchhand. There could be an army hidden in there.

But what the FAC had us bombing was anyone's guess.

Shackler bent back around and made another pass, dropped the rest of his bombs and then broke it off, climbing back to altitude. Randy Wayne eased up into formation with us.

"What'd we hit?" I asked.

"Jungle," Shackler said.

The FAC called, "Duke Lead, this is Fat Cat. Ready to copy BDA?"

"Roger, Fat Cat. Go."

"No confirmed battle damage due to smoke and jungle. How about sixty percent target coverage?"

"Roger," Shackler said, "a fair assessment." Then on intercom he said, "Hell, we got those bastards, I don't care what he says."

He hummed to himself and leveled off. "Don't worry about it. If it's dead, it was VC. That's the trouble with Lebowitz."

I waited.

"You gotta learn to turn it off. He knows that, but he can't." Humming. "A man'll lose his nuts if he doesn't. Can you see what we just bombed?"

He banked the plane suddenly and I looked down. Jungle. "No."

Humming. He shallowed the bank for a slow three-sixty turn. "A man's gotta go on."

"He thinks he killed those kids," I said.

"Hell, he was just trying to save them. A man can live with that."

We finished the mission and were down and debriefed by noon. At the hootch I found the bedroom sweet with musk and smoke and wine. An alto saxophone humped out heat music on the stereo. The room was dark, the shades drawn, and in the corner an electric fan stirred the hot air.

Then I saw them on Croom's bed, Hannah in a halter and hot pants, Croom with a shirt, his Goliath legs stuck out behind her and cradling her shoulders with one arm. She inhaled, her eyes lost in darkness, her cigarette star glowing.

I turned to go.

"Hey, man," Croom called loud over the saxophone. "We need you here."

"Hey, Moose!" Lebowitz called drunkenly.

"Lebowitz," I answered and waved. Hannah smiled and Croom let her go.

"Hannah," Lebowitz said, his voice slurring, his arms out. He kissed her on the cheek and she hugged him. His eyes were wild, the lids puffed. He shook his head and fell bouncing on the bed. His hands were limp at his sides, his mouth open.

Hannah took her cigarette and put it between his lips. He puffed, his eyes wide and red-rimmed, his gray hair flying like Moses' come down from the mountain.

"Tell you what," he said, the cigarette bouncing between his lips. "Let's have a party."

Croom grinned. "We're having a party, man."

"The hell you say," Lebowitz shouted. "Look at the Moose! He looks like he just lost his best friend. Cheer up, Moose, what the hell, baby! Hannah, get him some wine."

I picked up my glass, half-full, and showed it to him.

"Then drink!" Lebowitz cried. He jerked the cigarette out and threw it against the wall. He ran his fingers through his hair, but it was stiff and wild and kept rising up.

Hannah tipped her head toward him. She leaned close and kissed me, her lips moist, and brushed her cheek on mine.

"Talk to him," she whispered.

I sat down on the bed beside Lebowitz and sipped the wine, warm now, and after a while Lebowitz leaned back against the wall. He was breathing slowly through his mouth.

"Where you been?" he said quietly. "Flying?"

I nodded.

He breathed deeply for a while, his eyelids partially closed. When he spoke again his voice was dry, thin, high-pitched. "I'm through. I'll never fly again."

I didn't know what to say. I glanced over at Croom but he had closed his eyes, although I was sure he was listening.

"What do you think of that?" Lebowitz said.

"It's up to you."

"'It's up to you.' That's what Croom says. What kind of advice is that?" He wiped his lips so hard I thought they'd bleed.

"Colonel Dodd won't let you quit," Croom said.

"Let him shove it," Lebowitz said, standing up.

"Play cool," Croom said, his smile broad. "Back off, if he starts to crucify you. And he will. Tell him you'll fly. Then find a nice empty area like a Ranchhand trail so you can see no one's down there, and dump everything. Tell them you missed."

Lebowitz stood swaying and glaring at Croom. Finally he turned away and hissed something under his breath. He began to drink again, rapidly, five or six glasses of wine fast as he could pour them. Hannah sat on the bed and stroked his hair, and later she laid his head down and kissed him and he slept.

I needed to talk to someone, but Croom had gone with Hannah, and it was late. So I found the cassette and went downstairs near the bunker and began another report in the dark. Nothing would come. I shut off the mike and listened. I heard heavy bombing not far away, probably one of the villages. The NVA must have taken it over, to bring on such attacks. I hated to think about what the villages would look like if the F-4s had to bomb them out.

Steadily, the end was coming. All those reports of supplies and reinforcements for the final offensive must be true. After a while the heaviest concussions stopped. I flicked on the mike again but could think of nothing I wanted to say.

Lebowitz came along to breakfast because Croom made him, but he ate nothing and looked sick with bile. He seemed ten years older and pounds thinner. He had shaved and nicked himself in several places. He said little, looked no one in the eye, and left before the rest of us. Malatesta stopped by our table right after he left and asked if Lebowitz would be ready for the mission. Croom told him yeah, he thought so.

And he was. Croom told me later that when Lebowitz tried to ground himself Colonel Dodd threatened a court-martial. Croom said Lebowitz played it cool, though, claimed he was just tired, and agreed to fly. He and Malatesta went up together on the late morning mission.

At noon I ran three miles and showered, and when I was changing clothes I heard them on the stairs. Malatesta was halfway up the stairs, his flight suit clinging to him. He never looked back at Lebowitz, who climbed slowly behind him, his gray hair matted, his eyes hollow.

"You watch me!" Malatesta said, his voice hoarse as if he had been screaming all the way from the flight line.

Lebowitz answered him, his voice hollow as his eyes. "Tell anyone you like," he said. "You can't prove a thing."

"You watch me," Malatesta repeated, whirling around at the top of the stairs. "After I shower I'm going to Colonel Dodd and the IG. Wasting those bombs in the jungle. You've had it this time, Granny."

"Eat it," Lebowitz said, reaching the top step.

Malatesta grabbed his arm. Lebowitz whirled and flung his hand away. Crouched, he looked the same height as Malatesta but easily fifty pounds lighter.

Malatesta took a step back, his thick face grinning slowly. "Oh," he said. "Baby-killer wants to play rough, does he?"

Lebowitz crouched, his eyes wild. Malatesta made a rush and slammed Lebowitz against the wall. Lebowitz fell dazed, trying to get up. He swung and Malatesta backed away.

I saw Croom out of the corner of my eye. He seemed to

float up the stairs, no sound, and spun Malatesta around.

"This ain't none of your fight," Malatesta warned, trying to jerk away.

Croom lifted him by the butt and collar of the flight suit. Malatesta flailed at him, but Croom walked a couple of steps to the rail and held Malatesta out at arms' length, two stories up. Croom was glistening with sweat, in black gym shorts, his arms bulging.

"All right, all right!" Malatesta said. He stopped struggling and hung there like a giant sea turtle held over a cliff. "I'll leave him alone."

Croom hauled him in and set him on the porch. Malatesta stormed off to his room, heaving, his collar stretched up where Croom had held him.

"Find a nice Ranchhand trail?" Croom asked.

Lebowitz walked over and leaned on the rail. "A burned-out field. I said I saw someone running through it."

"And he was gonna turn you in?" Croom said, grinning.

"Yes, and he ought to!" He slammed his fist into the post.

"Easy," Croom said.

His fist hung twitching. "It didn't do any good," he said.

"Neither would a court-martial," Croom said. "Go on and fly. Malatesta will leave you alone, now."

Lebowitz put his head down on the rail. "Hell," he wept. "Oh, hell."

But Croom was wrong. Next morning, Lebowitz and Malatesta had been up less than an hour when we heard cursing on Guard Channel.

"The son of a bitch did it again!" Malatesta's voice blasted over the command set.

"Malatesta," the controller contacted him, "you're on Guard Channel."

"I know that! Any aircraft in the Pimah area, this is Random One. Need confirmation of a wasted bomb drop in a clear zone about twenty south of Pimah Mountain."

A pause, then Malatesta's voice blasted again, the volume high. "Pilot is Lebowitz, the baby-killer of Bien Dien. He's turned from the dump zone and is returning to base. Request pilot confirmation of fresh bomb strike in the open at coordinates Kilo-234.8 and Zulu-94.2."

"Now he's done it," a pilot said softly.

In front of the Operations Center there were soon two or three dozen standing around watching the skies. I joined them to wait for Lebowitz. Someone said something and another laughed, but mostly they were quiet. It was hot and thunderstorms were building in the west.

"Here they come," someone said, pointing.

I could see the Phantom low over the horizon and still miles out, lower than a normal approach. As it came nearer someone said, "He's coming straight in."

Soon we saw the landing gear spread down as the aircraft skimmed along over the trees off the approach end of the runway. The aircraft cleared the trees and dropped toward the approach lights, rounding out and holding, and just as it crossed the runway the pilot seemed to spike it down. It bounced, one wing low, leveled and touched again, hurtling down the runway. Still going fast, the F-4 dumped its nose again and again as Lebowitz pumped the brakes. Then the canopies started to open, and as the aircraft approached the midpoint Lebowitz threw his helmet away and climbed out of the cockpit.

"He's gone crazy," someone said.

Hanging on to the canopy rail, Lebowitz made his way along to the rear cockpit. The aircraft kept rolling on the runway at fifty or sixty knots. Lebowitz reached the rear and began beating at Malatesta with his fist, hanging on to the rail with one hand and pounding as fast as he could with the other. Then, as if Malatesta had hit him with a two-by-four, Lebowitz fell clear of the plane and crashed to the runway on his back. His body bounced and rolled and then lay still. The F-4 slowed and Malatesta turned off onto the taxiway and stopped.

I ran for the crash truck just as it pulled out, the siren screaming. I held tight as it left the ramp and sped across the field. A corpsman and I hit the ground running as the truck wheeled up and stopped next to him. Lebowitz lay twisted and his face was bleeding. One leg was doubled under itself and he lay stiff with his back arched, as if a knife were under him. His eyes were open and he focused on the corpsman and his lips started to work. Blood from his head oozed out and pooled on the concrete, streaked black with tire marks.

"Don't move him," the corpsman said, holding his shoulders.

Another corpsman ran up with a stretcher and placed it beside him.

Lebowitz rolled his eyes and saw me. "Moose," he said. "I didn't mean to do it."

The corpsmen raised him carefully and I slid the stretcher under, and all the way to the hospital the siren rose and fell, rose and fell like an air raid siren stuck open and wailing long after the attack.

WAITING FOR THE END

ROBERT E. LEE
NEVER FLEW JETS

What I remember about Randy Wayne is a shy, halfhearted smile, as if he had almost everything he had ever wanted. Later, after he was shot down north of Da Nang and forty gunships night and day tried to rescue him, I kept thinking about my first flight with him, my first month in Vietnam.

I found him in the pilots' lounge, sipping coffee and smoking. He nodded when he saw me come in. "Be with you in a minute," he said, his eyes clear, lazy as always. He tasted his lower lip slowly, as if almost asleep. His eyes were on the far wall.

I took a chair beside him and looked at the wall. There was a color blow-up, ten by twenty feet, of a Phantom climbing, a line of thunderstorms in the distance. I had heard the F-4 was the greatest fighter plane ever built. Old pilots who hadn't flown fighters since World War II wrote buddies in the Pentagon begging to be upgraded in it. Phantom pilots often passed up cushy assignments to exotic places just to have one more year in the aircraft, anywhere in the world.

That was the look in Randy's eyes, now, as he sat in the lounge with his legs crossed, sipping the last of his coffee, near the end of his third tour in Nam, watching the blow-up of his F-4 on the wall. Like a design on a Grecian urn, the Phantom there and in his mind would fly on in power and grace forever.

Randy held up his empty mug and a Vietnamese maid hurried over and took it. "Thank you," he said softly.

She bowed and smiled at him, a tiny girl with long black hair, a scar on her face like a birthmark or a burn. "Thank you, Captain Wayne."

He watched her go away to wash the mug, half-smiling like a man approving his teenage daughter doing her chores.

Randy Wayne was not my idea of a hero. At the officers' club, Wayne sat there quiet and unimposing while people like Shackler roared on and on about the war. While Shackler tanked up on Scotch and water, Randy nursed a single beer which must have gone flat before he had taken three sips. Shackler slid his hand up the slit skirts of all the bar girls waiting our tables, but Randy Wayne hardly seemed to notice they were there. Once he smiled at one, a halfhearted old man's smile. He never cursed, never threatened to beat the hell out of anyone. He didn't tell war stories, didn't use his hands to explain flying maneuvers, or damn the State Department for restricting the North Vietnam targets to be bombed.

Five-ten and flaccidly handsome, he had the weary, contented look of someone who knew exactly what his place in life was and had long ago quit worrying about it. Said to be the best pilot in Vietnam, he was only a captain, although that didn't seem to bother him. According to Lebowitz, he was married with two children, and was over thirty. When President Kennedy was assassinated, Randy had dropped out of law school and joined Officer Training School. Flying gave his life meaning, although he never saw combat until 1967. Now he was on his third combat tour, and in all he had shot down three MiGs and had flown almost three hundred missions.

A gentleman by birth and bearing, he would have looked good in portraits. But whenever he stood up, I noticed that for all his good looks he carried a stomach low at his belt line, like an underinflated basketball. He had probably always had it. His flesh was weak, only the spirit firm. When he left the officers' club, he never gestured grandly the way Shackler did, but simply etched that half-smile and said good night, as if we had known each other well for years, or as if we would never get better acquainted than we were at that moment. I found it hard to imagine him as the one controlling that jet fighter so smoothly three feet away from our wing tip each time I went up with Shackler, or to imagine Randy a hero of actual combat, to think of that frail body flying supersonic.

But even Shackler said he was the best in the wing. Crew chiefs gambled with each other for the right to have him fly their plane.

Randy turned to me. "Ready?"

"Anytime," I said.

On the way to the F-4 he briefed me on the mission, a routine cover flight. The takeoff was not much different from Shackler's, maybe a little smoother. The speed stunned me so much on every takeoff that I was aware of little else than being forced back in the seat, the runway racing by and the sudden calm after lift-off, the green jungle falling away as if we were heading for orbit.

But from the first break out of traffic, I could feel the difference. A swift, clean roll-in with the controls so well coordinated I didn't feel my body tugged away from the turn, only a gradual heaviness of the G-forces, like a massage. And no humming, as Shackler always did.

The morning sun burst brilliant in the canopy as he bent back around to the east, level at three thousand. He kept easing the throttle back and we passed over the nearest village at under three hundred knots. In no time we crossed a stream that was almost hidden by trees. The stream coiled along more winding than a trail, a slow, shimmering creek with rice paddies patched along its banks. Several thatched roofs appeared in a clearing.

"That's Co Mihn," Randy said.

"VC village?"

"Right. Another one back on the far side of the road."

He rolled into a one-eighty, coasting low until we were skimming the trees. The jungle raced by like a blur. I tried aiming my eyes in little jumps several hundred meters ahead.

He added power and began to climb, and the jungle dropped away underneath.

"Moose, go button seven."

"Roger," I said, and heard the radio whir as it changed from the TOC frequency.

I heard a battle in progress, the air filled with chatter, like all other flights with Shackler. I still couldn't make sense of most of it, but Randy banked immediately to the west and leveled at ten thousand, throttle open.

He called, "Duke, roger your message. Rivet here, forty east, single, full wet with rockets."

"Roger, Randy," I heard Shackler's voice acknowledge. "I could use some help. Bu Cai's getting hit hard and I'm dry. Shot up a wad of them, but they keep coming. Looks like a major assault. Camp commander radioed heavy casualties and then broke contact. I'll orbit low and slow and draw their fire till you get here."

"Roger, be there in three minutes. Going TOC channel for more help. Take care."

The radio whirred and cleared. "Watchdog, Rivet, over."

"Go ahead, Rivet," the base answered.

"Watchdog, Duke reports Bu Cai under heavy assault. He's dry and orbiting till I arrive in about two minutes. Request urgent scramble and choppers for dust-off of casualties."

"Roger, Rivet. Help's on the way."

When the radio cleared back to Shackler's channel, we heard him in the middle of a transmission.

". . . about ten north. I'll eject at a thousand feet so maybe they won't potshot me. Over."

"Duke, say again, are you hit?"

"That's affirm," Shackler said, his voice calm. "I'm milking it north away from the heaviest weapon fire. How about a dust-off?"

"On its way, Norm. Okay, I have you in sight. Stay put after you land."

"Roger. Here goes."

Randy slid the throttle back and the Phantom surged and I felt it slowing. Down ahead of us I saw the orange and white panels of the parachute billow, low above the trees, and then a bright fireball as the F-4 crashed less than a mile away.

Randy set up a spiral around the parachute, steepening the descent when the chute collapsed in the trees. At a thousand feet he leveled off, circling, and in a few minutes he began the cannon fire, short bursts bracketing the spot where Shackler disappeared.

"Rivet, this is Dust-off One, directions."

"Roger, One," Randy answered, easy, spacing his cannon bursts between phrases. "Proceed red-lined ten nautical miles north of Bu Cai. Duke has punched out and is ready for pickup."

"Roger, give us five. Any enemy contact?"

"A few," Randy said. "I'll cover till you make rescue."

In a few minutes the chopper arrived and hovered and drew him out with a jungle penetrator. Throughout, Randy kept his rhythm, weaving in and out of a pattern, tempting the VC gunners who had converged on the site, and whenever they opened up on us he bent around and blasted them with cannon bursts or, if they were far enough away from Shackler, with rockets.

When the chopper lifted away and dashed south low above the jungle toward the Special Forces camp, Randy banked and raced past it. He brought us up to five thousand feet and even before I could see the camp I knew he had a target.

"All right," he said, "turn your oxygen regulator to a hundred percent, in case we get hit, and rest your hands on your thighs."

I did as he said, waiting. Suddenly, the nose dropped smoothly and steadily and the first rockets shot ahead. Instantly he dropped the nose even lower and fired two cannon bursts, then pulled hard and the flash of explosions shot up on both sides.

"Good shot, Rivet," someone called. "Rover One with a buddy here to assist."

"Roger," Randy said, already dropping out of a wingover for another pass. "Try the south quadrant and if you don't raise any fire you might cover the dust-off sliding in from the north."

"Roger, and two more dust-offs are on the way."

On the second pass I could see tracers coming up away from the sun, streams of automatic fire like an orange chain link fence, and suddenly I was afraid. There's no way, I thought, but then we were in it and I saw our rockets flash away and felt the bombs release. There was a thud behind us as if we had run over a dog on the highway.

"You okay?" Randy said, pulling up, the sky above us blue and safe.

I glanced down at my hands, clutched protectively at my loins. "I guess so. Are we?"

"Took a few hits. No signs of damage, though."

I watched several other Phantoms arrive and begin blasting away at the jungle, not nearly as low as we had been, but risking the tracers reaching up at them.

"We're out of ammo," Randy said. "If it's okay with you, we'll make a few dry passes while the dust-offs pick up casualties at the camp. Looks like they might have to evacuate everyone. They're pretty well shot up."

"Sure," I said, but scared to death, thinking of that wall of fire, scared too of Randy, who had done this so often he didn't seem to weigh the risks, anymore. I wondered if he had forgotten the options, that a man could be a doctor or lawyer and live longer. Long life was the furthest thing from his mind, now. He flew with gun-barrel vision, as if nothing in the world mattered but flying.

Here in his Phantom, he was first among the finest, more powerful than any other profession could make him. No, that wasn't it. In his first combat tour, his job was to hunt and shoot down MiGs. Now, it was to keep as many men on the ground alive as he could until the dust-offs could rescue them. The years between now and old age must have seemed a waste of effort compared to this way of life, even this risk of death. An F-4 had been his Harvard, and Vietnam his Yale. History books proudly record Lee's humane remark to an aide during the battle of Fredericksburg: "It's a good thing war is so terrible, or men would come to love it too much." But unlike Randy Wayne, Robert E. Lee never flew jets.

Randy circled the camp and tracers blurred and made me dizzy until I almost forgot they were real, and I watched in fascination while the chopper with Shackler settled down and loaded casualties. It lifted off and swung north, away from the heaviest fire, and as if on cue, two other Search and Rescue choppers whirled down and hovered. Other F-4s arrived and blasted the VC positions, and still we circled, tracers seeking us all the way, and then the last chopper lifted off and labored away.

"Rover One," Randy called, "Rivet is bingo on fuel. Returning to base."

"Roger, Randy. Good show."

We were three hundred feet over the camp, pushing the Mach needle, and Randy stood the Phantom on its wing tip, pulling around in a tight five-G turn. I looked straight down at the jungle, feeling a touch of the glory Randy must feel every time he flew. Down in the green, arcing across the trees like a boomerang, a thin swathe of colors sliced along our flight path. I saw Randy looking behind us and I craned my neck and looked back. Pressure contrails swirled off the lower wing tip in the humid air, swirling a rainbow to the sun.

WHY RANDY WAYNE CRASHED AND BURNED

The first time he saw it, he was sure it was a joke. But when he switched on the light and saw the blood, he knew it was real.

Since then he had seen it many times. Appearing soon after his pilot training squadron's first accident, it usually sat quietly in a corner, in dim light. A burned pilot, fatally mangled in a crash, it made little noise and never left blood on the chair. Its feet were burned away to the boot tops, the flight suit covered with gore squeezed through rips in the material. It wore what remained of a jet crash helmet, the blackened shell twisted down over the dark bloody meat that had been its face.

It was often there, sprawled in a dark corner of his room. He wondered if it showed itself to any of the others. It appeared to him anywhere, at odd times, listening to their fun, amused by their boasts. At a really nasty joke or a war story someone repeated from an instructor pilot, Randy could hear it laughing, choked with blood, an empty, head-thrown-back laugh gurgling out of the mangled cavern that had been its mouth.

Randy had never been afraid of death before. From the start of pilot training, he found himself enjoying the physical danger. Every part of training was aimed at making them into heroes. They learned to leap into a pool in full flight gear and swim underwater to escape an oil fire, as if they had crashed at sea. They learned to eat snakes and evade patrols in the South Georgia swamps. They learned judo, karate, and how to slit a man's throat.

"Kill that bastard!" the sergeant with the cropped hair said. "You're a pilot down in the jungle. He's a commie son with a bayonet. You ain't never gonna fly anymore if he cuts you with it!"

So they learned to lunge and almost beat each other to death with pugil sticks, all so they could live to fly.

The stubby T-28 they flew had a wing span of forty feet, and a thousand-horsepower radial engine. The huge convex canopy bulged high over the thick fuselage, and when Randy glanced over his shoulder during a spin, he saw the tall, nearly rectangular rudder twenty feet away banging like a barn door in a storm.

Then came the first accident. They were outside the ready room and someone yelled, "Look out!"

A T-28 zoomed low toward the base, dark smoke squirting down behind it. Randy stood helpless while the aircraft dropped near the tree line.

"Come on, come on!" someone said.

The aircraft seemed to leap back into the air, cleared the trees, and settled again toward the field. Flames shot out, bright orange bursting through the trailing smoke. The pilot leveled off and held it, the fire flowing from the dead engine. The aircraft hung there with its propeller straight across, and Randy could hear the flames whipping like wind through a cavern.

The gear held up despite the hard impact, and even while the aircraft rolled, the canopy slid back and both pilots climbed out onto the wing and ran to the wing tip and leaped off, tumbling away while the aircraft rolled on in flames, two fire trucks racing toward it.

The two men got up running and the flight line went wild,

everyone yelling and beating each other on the back. They shook their fists and shouted, "Did you see that? Hot damn, did you see that!"

Late that night, when Randy returned from the officers' club where they had told each other the story for the hundredth time, proud of their first shared danger, he could feel the thrill trailing him like smoke whipping away from the plane. He couldn't take it all in, and his heart raced.

After midnight, he was studying at his desk when he felt it for the first time. It came over him slowly, a sense of devastation that began in his feet and burned its way up his back to the top of his skull. Staring at the wall, Randy snapped his eyes down at the flight manual and searched for his place. He tried to read, but he felt someone watching him.

He shoved the swivel chair around and shuddered. The mutilated corpse sprawled in the far corner. It's a joke, he thought, and stumbled to flip on the ceiling light. But he saw the blood clearly and stood still, tingling. The stench of jet fuel and burned flesh made him gag. The back of his skull felt scalped. He had a vision of himself crashing someday—a captain, perhaps, or a major—horribly mangled, trapped in a crushed cockpit, burning to death.

He passed his hand over his face and hurried outside across the street to the club, where he found four of his friends remaining. He drank with them until two, when the sergeant tending bar turned out the lights.

At times, Randy almost asked if others were ever afraid, but he couldn't bring himself to risk it. There were some things you didn't confess in the military. Three lieutenants had already washed out of his class because of the demon, fear of flying. Shamed, they never came to the club, and tried to stay out of sight until they could be reassigned some place forgettable.

Nights, Randy found it waiting for him there in the corner, although sometimes, logged with alcohol, he could stare at the corner and fear nothing. But even then, he never knew when he might hear as he fell asleep something like laughter, hollow and mocking, faraway.

On Tuesday, he was the fourth one to solo, a neat, tight takeoff and landing that made his instructor grin when Randy taxied back to the ramp and shut down.

"Grease job!" his buddies shouted, and wrapped the white scarf around his neck. They beat him on the back and he smiled.

Fired with wonder, Randy slipped off on his second solo the next day with another student. South of the base, they slid down beneath the three-thousand-foot minimum and leveled off above the trees, chasing each other with a feeling of power like nothing Randy had ever known.

That night, Randy dreamed something and sat up suddenly in bed. His scalp ached with the vision. He kept seeing his plane clip a limb and cartwheel in flames in the trees. In the warm Georgia night, he drew up the woolen blanket and closed his eyes.

For days, it appeared to him everywhere. At the club during happy hour, Randy seemed to be the only one who saw it leaning on the bar next to him, the face butchered, the demolished crash helmet dangling a ruptured oxygen hose like an esophagus ripped from its throat.

By Saturday, he felt drugged from loss of sleep. That night, though, the squadron threw a party for everyone who had soloed, and by midnight they were wild to be heroes forever. All night they could say anything about their instructors to their faces and get away with it. The instructor pilots sat at their tables with the sleek, unruffled poise of proven tigers. Nothing could touch them, and they showed it. Their students knew it, and they gave all their insults in fun and envy, and they toasted each other and shouted jokes above the loud beat of the combo.

At midnight they began lighting blue blazers, a shot of

brandy touched by a match to make a slow blue flame waver on top. Each man threw back his head and tossed it down, as if swallowing the flames in defiance. Each drank the number of his turn to solo. Fourth, Randy downed his four blazers to cheers and catcalls. He found the blue flames exciting, and he munched them one by one like dares. And he grinned at his buddies downing their ten, their twelve blue flames throughout the night, the whole squadron getting drunk on courage.

On Monday, he took off on his third solo. He practiced chandelles and rolls until he believed he could do them with his eyes closed. Then he climbed back up, looked carefully to clear the area, and slowed the aircraft to practice stalls. Raising the nose as the airspeed died, he rolled in back-trim and held the throttle, ready. The wing tips burbled and the shudder of the stall began, and just as the left wing dropped, Randy shoved the throttle forward—and the engine failed.

He released stick pressure and let the nose drop through the stall. The engine backfired, and he jerked the throttle to idle. Nose down, the aircraft began flying again, but downward, powerless, the negative G-forces nudging him up against the shoulder harness. The Georgia fields five thousand feet below loomed greener every second.

He eased in the throttle and now the engine responded, and he led the nose up with back pressure, climbing with the throttle open. The horizon fell past the cockpit again, and the blue sky opened ahead of him. He climbed slowly and checked the airspeed, one-twenty, one-thirty, one-forty-five. He kept the throttle open until high cruise speed, then eased off and thought hard about what to do.

He cross-checked the fuel gauge and the oil pressure. Both fine. The hydraulic pressure, okay. Maybe there's nothing wrong, he thought.

He shifted taller in the seat and eased back the throttle

only halfway, then brought it all the way back to idle. He held the nose level, and as the airspeed dropped, he felt the control stick growing mushy in his fist. His back crawled, as if someone was watching him from behind. The airspeed fell through one-forty, one-thirty-five.

Approaching the stall, Randy fought the urge to glance at the empty rear cockpit. He waited, trying to feel the first tremors lighter than ghost fingers on the controls, the first sign of a stall coming on. The engine, idling, hammered and popped like laughter, louder as the airspeed fell. The stick came back in his hand and the wing tips fluttered, and the nose plunged downward.

Randy shoved in the throttle, and the engine missed and banged and cut out as if it had died.

Then he heard it, the hollow laughter, howling behind him in the rear cockpit. His face blazed with fear. He shoved the stick forward to avoid a spin and mashed both feet on the rudder pedals. The wings began flying again and the shuddering stopped.

Fist tight, he nudged the throttle up an inch and the engine sputtered and died away. Fighting panic, he fed in another inch and felt the engine pound and take hold and force him back in the seat. Another inch, and the engine surged, and he began to climb.

He couldn't hear it now above the engine roar, but he felt it mocking him, the laughter screaming out of the cavern of its mouth.

Climbing, he cross-checked everything again. Nothing seemed in the red. It has to be the spark plugs, he thought. But he knew it could be something worse. What if a fuel line ruptured and sprayed fuel over the hot engine and caught fire? He thought briefly of bailing out and letting the doomed aircraft crash. But no, he couldn't do that.

He would have to make an emergency landing pattern, he

decided, and let the mechanics have a look at it. If they found nothing wrong, if his instructor chewed him out and everyone thought he was chicken, he didn't know what he'd do. He thought of ignoring it and making a normal landing pattern. But if the engine cut out again, he might drop too low and crash into the Georgia pines off the approach end of the runway and, like the ghost in the helmet, burn.

He had to risk the shame. It was not even good flying sense to make a normal pattern with a bad engine. That meant going to Cleburne, the small airstrip where they practiced landings.

Banking toward Cleburne, he made the call. "Dobbs tower, this is Bearcat Two-Three."

Instantly an instructor's voice answered, calm, professional. "Two-Three, this is Dobbs tower, go ahead."

"Dobbs, Bearcat Two-Three has engine malfunction, proceeding to Cleburne for emergency landing."

A slight pause. Then, "Roger, Two-Three. Are you declaring Mayday?"

"Negative," Randy said, but wishing he could declare a full emergency. "The engine cut out on me twice, but it's running, now."

"Roger, Two-Three. Proceed to Cleburne and start a three-sixty overhead letdown. Do you know your procedure and altitudes?"

"Yes, sir," Randy said.

"Repeat them, Two-Three."

"High point at six thousand feet," Randy recited, "midpoint, forty-five hundred, base at three. Turn final, no less than fifteen hundred."

"That's affirmative, Two-Three. Watch your round out and have a smooth touchdown. We'll have a bird over for you in half an hour."

Randy reached Cleburne at six thousand feet and set up

the spiral, passing midpoint in a tight pattern, too high. He shallowed the bank and hit base point exactly and turned final with a hundred feet to spare. All the way down, the engine, set on a thousand RPMs, hummed perfectly. He reached round out and cut the power, holding it off, off, and touched at the first intersection. Just as he had practiced.

He taxied in and turned onto the ramp and sat there in the high canopy, idling for a minute, waiting. Late in the day, there was no one on duty, so he cut the engine and got out to chock the wheels.

He touched the cowling and jerked his burned hand away, shaking his fingers, and stared up at the engine. He wondered how anything so big could misfire. That anything so big could actually fly was still a wonder to him.

Searching the burnished cowling for oil smears, for any signs of trouble, Randy felt dwarfed by the tons of metal. He discovered two broken rivets, oil leaks in three places, and a suspicious line on the propeller blade that might become a dangerous crack. The aircraft seemed no more now than just potential bits of wreckage.

He heard something at his back and turned to see another T-28 hurrying to land. The pilot didn't bother with a usual pattern, but slipped the aircraft through a tight turn and eased level just above the runway. The wheels held off, then kissed down firmly and the pilot quickly braked and turned off at the first intersection. A postage-stamp landing, with less than a thousand-foot roll. Whoever they sent to pick him up could fly.

There was a master sergeant already climbing out of the cockpit as the aircraft taxied up and spun around next to Randy's. Randy snapped to attention, for the pilot was Colonel Wren, the Wing Commander. He closed the throttle and vaulted out onto the wing, his flight cap shining with the eagle insignia.

Randy saluted and the colonel tossed a return.

"All right, son," he said, his voice sharp but not angry. "What's the trouble?"

"I'm not sure, sir. Spark plugs fouled, I'd guess."

The colonel nodded and leaped to the ground. He was shorter than Randy, lean, a man in his early forties who had flown hundreds of combat missions in World War II and Korea. He sported a pale mustache that matched the color of his eyebrows, and his face was lean with hard golden skin, like bright copper.

"Brief me," he said, stripping off his gloves.

And while Randy told him about the flight, the engine trouble, and his decision to land at Cleburne, the mechanic opened the cowl flap and began to search.

In minutes he came over with his hands cupped. "Colonel Wren?" the mechanic said. "Three of them." He held up one of the spark plugs for them to see. "Caked with crud."

The colonel took it and turned it in the light. "Look at this, lieutenant," he said. "A pilot needs every ounce of power near the ground, or up in a tight turn with a bad guy on his tail. Plugs like this can kill you."

He handed the plug back and began stretching his gloves on again. "Good job, lieutenant."

Randy's heart surged. "Thank you, sir," he said. That was all he needed. He felt vindicated and proud, ready to fly the aircraft back, bad plugs and all.

Colonel Wren slapped him on the shoulder. "Come on, I'll give you a lift. The sergeant will clean the plugs and fly her back later."

Randy followed the colonel up and strapped into the rear cockpit. He sensed the precision in everything the colonel did. The colonel cranked up and started taxiing even before Randy had his headset on. The late afternoon sun was low, and they swung directly into it out to the end of the runway, where the colonel wheeled the nose sharply around into the crosswind and set the brakes. He ran the engine up and began making power checks before takeoff, grounding the magnetos to check the RPM drop.

There was a red convertible coming down the dirt road just beyond the wire fence, and the boy driving slid to a halt past their prop wash. The girl with him was laughing, her bright teeth showing, and she raised her hand above the windshield and waved. Randy nodded and lifted his gloved hand in salute. The boy returned his salute, his smile twisted with envy.

Thrilled by the moment, Randy wished he could keep this feeling forever, wished he were out there with them, filming this takeoff. It seemed one of the glorious events in history, with his white scarf fluttering around his neck, a famous pilot in the front cockpit sharing time with him, the engine roaring, and the twilight sky above.

Suddenly the girl stood up above the windshield and snapped a picture of the plane. He wanted to kiss her for that, wished he had a copy of the print, felt somehow a great loss, as if leaving an important glimpse of himself there in that black box. This moment was worth whatever waited for him. It would be months before he won his wings, but he knew now that he was meant to fly.

"All set?" the colonel's voice came over the intercom, a shared message between crewmen.

"Roger," he replied, and felt the canopy closing above him. "Ready to roll."

"Then off we go," the colonel said, swinging the nose directly down the runway.

The canopy shut out all sound but the rich mellow roar of the engine, muffled by the headset. Releasing the brakes, the colonel nudged the throttle all the way forward, and the black runway crawled by underneath, sliding, then hurtling faster and faster.

Randy let the force weld him to the seat. The power of the engine surged through his feet and fired his body with pride, and his face burned with the thrill, the immediate speed of flight.

He threw back his head and breathed deeply, a feeling of solitary delight that tumbled out in silent laughter, a laugh that resounded long, a bold feeling of valor that shook and possessed him down to his booted feet.

MAYDAY

I remember that the flag was at half-mast. Inside the Operations Center, a sergeant said Captain Wayne's crew chief had lowered it and threatened to kill any son of a bitch who raised it. From the looks of those around, though, no one would touch it. Several pilots turned to glare at me when I entered, their jaws tight. Everyone had killing in his eyes.

It had been confirmed. They had found Randy Wayne in the plane, what was left of it. A helicopter was on the way back with the body bag. It seemed incredible, since only last week I had flown with him.

I heard a flight of F-4s scream into the traffic pattern and pitch out one by one. Most of us went outside to watch. After they landed, a three-ship formation with an empty slot for the missing pilot roared over low and slow. I heard someone weeping, and no one looked anyone in the eye.

The first F-4s rolled slowly onto the ramp while the last three entered the pattern and pitched out and landed. A staff car met Colonel Dodd at his plane, and he and a captain sped away off the ramp toward headquarters. Shackler stomped off the ramp, his fists clenched. He left his parachute and helmet in the cockpit, so I knew he was going up again. I moved out to meet him but he stormed past into the Center. Several of the other pilots closed around him and I followed them inside.

Someone brought Shackler a beer and he drained it and crushed the can in his hand. They relayed him another and he nursed it and leaned on the counter, talking low and using his other hand to show them how Randy had crashed. He had deep bags under his eyes and the beginnings of jowls, drooping shoulders and the patch over his right zipper-pocket of a squadron commander. I waited behind them, listening as best I could. Some of the pilots left for their planes, refueled by now, ready for the afternoon mission.

Shackler crushed the can and left it on the counter. He went to the latrine and hurried back, pulling on his gloves.

"Mind if I come along?" I asked. "Colonel Tydings wants a report on what happened to Bien Dien village last night."

"Flattened," he said with hate, as if he wished he could do it again. "The whole thing's burned to the ground."

He stopped and scowled at me. "All right, come on."

I ran to Personal Equipment for gear, and by the time I got to the plane, Shackler had one engine lit and was firing the second. I threw the parachute over the rail and climbed into the cockpit, strapping in as fast as I could.

Shackler released the brakes and raced across the ramp to the nearest taxiway. I double-checked my straps, then worked the shoulder harness and lap belt together and locked in.

He braked the Phantom hard on the taxiway, swinging wide toward the runway. "Ready?" he snapped over the intercom.

"All set."

He rammed the throttle forward for a running takeoff, swinging wide to the outside of the runway, and hurtled down the shimmering black-streaked concrete. The speed of F-4s stunned me on every takeoff. He held the nose down until a few knots past takeoff speed, then jerked us into the air, reaching steeply for altitude. I remember it was a few minutes till one.

He bent back around to the east and chopped the throttle, and we crossed a stream coiling between rice paddies. Bien Dien village appeared in the clearing. Suddenly, he dumped the left wing and pulled us around in a tight arc directly above it.

"Take a look," he said impatiently.

The village was a blackened patchwork of smoke and craters, most roofs only rubble. Many of the houses smoldered, smoke drifting over the bordering jungle.

I wondered how Colonel Tydings expected me to write anything worthwhile about this. A few pictures from the air would say it better.

"They tried to overrun it again last night," Shackler broke in. "Took away half the rescue force that was searching for Randy."

Shackler jerked the F-4 away from the village, shoved in full throttle and began to climb. With his wing man lost, Shackler blamed everyone. I guessed we were heading for the Ho Chi Minh Trail, where Randy Wayne had gone down.

By the time we passed twenty thousand feet, he made contact with Broadside, a Forward Air Controller he must have worked with before, for Shackler called him by name.

"Listen, Wally, I want Triple-A. Don't give me any water buffaloes or skinny old men or broken-down trucks. Nothing but antiaircraft, you hear?"

"Roger, Norm," the FAC said.

At twenty-seven thousand, Shackler leveled and raced on toward the Trail. The whole country was jungle, and from this altitude it seemed impenetrable.

"Duke One," the FAC called. His voice was so clear it could have been inside my own head. "I have contact for you about a mile north of Kilo intersection."

Shackler dropped his head to look at a chart. "Roger, Broadside, I'm about eight minutes out, letting down now. You sure you got guns there?" He pulled the throttles and let the nose fall.

"They threw everything at me but their silk pajamas," the FAC said, his voice cool.

Dropping through twenty thousand, Shackler cleared his cannon, a short burst. He broke into a song for the first time, humming loud and in short bursts between breaths.

At five thousand, we swooped down between mountain ranges into a valley, and I raised my sun visor and tried to focus down below.

"Broadside," Shackler called. "We're through five, mark your smoke."

"Roger, Duke, I see you coming. Chances are they do too with the sun on you like that. Watch about ten miles your one o'clock position."

I looked right of the nose and saw the rocket hit and spread smoke west of the Trail, a sharp brown swath cutting along the base of the mountains. A hail of tracers immediately spewed up at the OV-10, and the pilot jinked out of range, bucking and jerking away, leaving a straight run open for us.

Shackler didn't even fire on the first pass. He bore low and forced them to fire point-blank, making sure they were a serious target. On the pullout, I saw tracers go past.

Rolling out, Shackler kicked the rudder to line up quickly and fired a salvo of rockets. They raced out in front of us and impacted near the smoke. White flak burst in front of us. He held us low over the trees for a three-count, then released bombs and pulled up hard. The bombs impacted and kicked us along and I thought we were hit. But he jammed the stick into my knee in a tight turn inside the mountains, and suddenly there was flak again at point-blank range.

"Wally!" Shackler screamed. "Why didn't you tell me about the Triple-A site up the mountain!" He finished the turn and dropped low over the Trail to escape.

I saw the OV-10 hanging above us near the mountain peak.

"Sorry, Duke," he called. "It just now opened up. Orbit, and I'll mark it for you."

"Shove it," Shackler said, zooming past the OV-10 and out over the top of the mountain. He passed the gun emplacement and I saw it, a set of short barrels camouflaged in the trees and exposed for a second.

He rolled out far from the Trail and began a gentle dive, head-on with the guns. Automatic weapon fire like an orange stream from a garden hose rose lazily to meet us. In a flash of horror I felt what Kamikaze pilots must have felt, strapped in, committed.

Rockets slid down and away, and flak burst out to meet us. Shackler pulled hard on the stick and I almost blacked out, but felt a jolt and heard a slashing sound. There was a burst of wind and something warm on my face, blinding me. I heard a scream and wondered if it was mine. I wiped my eyes as the aircraft bounced violently through the sky.

"Wait!" I heard him shout. Wind roared into my helmet and I strained to hear him.

". . . Mayday, Wally! We're punching out!"

I wiped my face on the other sleeve. Light burst bright into my eyes and I stared at blood on my sleeves. I found a dry spot and wiped again, and I could see shards of the canopies overhead splashed with blood. I felt no pain and knew it had to be Shackler.

"Mosely," he called, "when I say go, get out of there!"

"Roger!" I shouted.

"And for God's sake, stick to me on the ground!"

I tried to see out, but my eyes squeezed shut again and I rubbed them. We were at a thousand feet and climbing, the engines sluggish and cutting out.

There was a burst and a rush of wind that almost tore my helmet away. It was like standing under a waterfall. Shackler must have said "Go!" for I saw his fist jerk upward, and the black pointed nose of the aircraft was already falling off toward the jungle.

I reached down for the ejection handle and shoved my head back and squeezed. The force shot me above the Phantom and left me facing nothing but blue sky. Quickly the seat began to tumble and I grabbed the armrests, still traveling at three hundred knots. The jungle was coming up quick, and I searched for a D-ring as blue sky swirled overhead. Then the chute opened automatically and snapped me out of the seat.

Far off beyond the stream I saw Shackler's chute coming down. I grabbed a riser and squeezed my legs together and kept tugging. When I cleared the trees I faced a rocky hill downwind and the stream off to the right, and then bushes rose up and I flexed my knees and crashed into them.

I lay still in the deep grass and listened. The guns were silent, and the hum of the OV-10 was distant, climbing away from our position. But anyone on the ground would have seen the crash. They were probably hunting us already.

Crouching low under branches, shoving my way through the thickest undergrowth, I headed for the stream, knowing Shackler went down somewhere on the other side. Every few steps I froze and listened. There was water running on the left, but I heard something else, a voice, not Shackler's. At the risk of losing the stream, I turned away quickly, running for a place to hide.

I found a boulder canopied by a limb thick with branches spreading out twenty feet on each side. The stone was slick, and I clawed my way up. At the top, the boulder was cracked, a wedge wide enough to burrow into. I pulled myself into it and lay in the dark, covered by leaves, my face against the stone that was almost cold. I stopped breathing and listened, hearing nothing but my own heart.

Spreading the leaves apart, I saw the bright panels of Shackler's parachute snarled in a tree across the river. He was not in the harness, which hung there thirty feet above the bank. Suddenly there was a burst of shooting and I dropped the branch and ducked.

A series of semiautomatic rifle fire rang out, and a louder blast of weapons that went on and on, with only brief pauses.

I heard the sharp thud of his .38, drowned at once in a burst of rifle fire.

I heard the roar of a spotter plane diving and a *thump* across the stream, then another. I raised a branch and saw smoke where the FAC had marked their position. That meant an air strike coming, and I hoped they wouldn't hit Shackler.

Then the first rockets burst, and an F-4 roared past skimming the trees. The blast was fifty yards from the smoke, but the next one hit close and scattered it. I ducked as pieces of fallout hailed down on the trees.

There were two F-4s at first, but as the attack wore on I counted as many as five Phantoms in the air. As they flashed over I could see tracers and hear automatic rifle fire between passes, and barrages of flak burst over the trees until the sky was dark over the river.

A chopper whirled into range, but the hail of gunfire was so fierce the chopper couldn't get close. I never even saw it, but heard it hovering and then backing away. There was a pause, then the streaking sound of an F-4 circling overhead, and the jet zoomed past and the stream exploded in flames. Napalm billowed orange over the water and crackled through the trees along the far bank, and rockets exploded seconds before another jet roared by, climbing.

Several times on crossing runs, they strafed the river and cannon shells zipped past me before I could duck. Then a bomb hit on the far bank and sprayed out over the water, a dud, I thought. But I noticed smoke clinging to the trees, like gas, and during the lull I could hear human voices moaning and retching in pain.

At the first whiff, I buried my nose in my hands and tried not to breathe whatever it was, to squeeze the air through my fist, but I gagged and rose to my knees. I coughed and gagged and began to retch. My body shook and I retched and felt myself urinate and couldn't stop. My insides were on fire, coiling and throwing me from side to side. I couldn't see and I felt my nose bleeding. Suddenly my bowels voided and my knees drew up under me and I dry-heaved until I passed out.

When I came to, my head pounded as if it would split and my stomach burned. Hours had passed, for it was dark, and there was moaning not far away. I bit my tongue to keep from screaming.

I heard bombs and antiaircraft fire, but deep, far away on another part of the Trail. At night, hidden under the leaves, I had no sense of direction, just a horrible thirst. I squeezed my head to keep from moaning. I wondered how many VC had been trapped in the fumes, and if any of them had gas masks. I spread the leaves quietly and saw the flashing of antiaircraft fire and bombs far off in the night. I felt fragile and doomed, felt the nausea coming again and lay my head down for it to pass.

I woke to gunfire. I could hear an OV-10 circling, but it was ground fire that had startled me. I opened my eyes and saw needles of light through the leaves. The shooting was somewhere else. I turned my head and sensed it was across the stream. It stopped and there was silence, then a sudden burst of gunfire and a scream.

Shackler. Another burst of fire, then silence.

A smoke rocket thumped and I heard a jet whining down from somewhere. The first jet made its pass and flak exploded overhead. A bomb ruptured with a brilliant flash, napalm again. I saw the jungle burst into flames beyond the stream, even a few trees blazing this side of the water.

At first I thought it was only my head pounding, but it got louder and louder and then through the leaves I saw a rescue chopper spill down over the line of trees and hover above the water. I saw the gunner in the doorway, his machine gun aimed downstream, another man leaning above him and looking upstream along the bank.

I pushed myself to my knees and paused, light-headed, about to pass out. I waited till I was steady, then clawed through the branches and tumbled heavily to the ground. I remember thinking someone would shoot me. But I heard the chopper and stood up and began to run toward the sound, crouching along under limbs, crashing through shrubs, certain that a squad of VC would be waiting in ambush.

The ground fell away to the stream and I saw the chopper hanging about fifty yards downstream. They were drawing heavy fire and backing off, their own guns spraying the jungle along both banks. I ran down the embankment, letting my momentum carry me into the clear. In blinding sunlight, I waved my arms and ran downstream toward them, but the chopper was taking too much fire and lurched away.

I turned and dived toward the webbed roots of a tree hanging over the water. Across the stream they raked the bank with bullets. I lay face down and felt my heart beating against the sand. I remember hearing the whine of a jet from far off, screaming lower and nearer and rushing past. I rolled away toward the tree as napalm exploded into flames on the other shore, so close I could hear flesh pop, and a flaming mass of napalm struck my face.

I screamed and clawed at my face and burned my hands. I rolled in the dirt and stumbled up running and dived for the river. I came up gasping for air and screaming, my face and neck on fire, my fists scraping at the flaming jelly. I heard the thudding chopper coming near and forced my eyes open. It was hovering high, dangling a jungle penetrator underneath on a cable. My eyes squeezed shut in pain and I held up my arms.

The seat hit me in the chest and I clutched it and felt my legs lift clear of the water. The chopper blades blasted down at me. I thought, I'll be shot, but I held on. I wouldn't have let go even if they killed me.

The whirring deepened and I sensed we were higher and going fast. Soon I felt hands reach out and grab my arms and haul me inside the cabin. The wind stopped but I held tight, even when I felt their hands trying to loosen my fingers. I remember I tried to open my eyes but couldn't.

"Jesus!" I heard someone say, and knew I was safe as I would ever be. "Look at his face!"

WAITING FOR
THE END

I knew by smell I had been there before, but I couldn't think where. Alcohol, or iodine. And something sweet, chloroform. I started to open my eyes but they hurt too much. I seemed to exist only from the neck up, and all of that was on fire. I remembered the napalm, the flash that burned and burned no matter how long I gouged and tried to wipe it away. I didn't remember a shot, but they must have knocked me out aboard the chopper, and now it was over. The hospital sheets felt crisp and my face blazed.

I squeezed my eyes open, but it was too bright and I clamped them shut again. I raised to one elbow, feeling heavy and drugged. Slowly, I hunched to sit up in the bed. I opened my eyes again, letting light burn in until I could stand it.

Through narrow slits, I saw beds of white, like shrouds, all down the surgical ward, some of them with blood soaking through.

"Christ!" I heard Lebowitz say. "You look like a mummy."

I turned and saw him stretched in traction on his bed, his eyes cut toward me.

His thin face was almost emaciated, his eyes squinted almost shut deep in dark sockets, as if in constant pain.

"That is you, isn't it, Moose?"

"Yeah," I mumbled, my voice muffled and faraway as if gagged. I raised my hands even with the slit of my eyes and saw them swathed thick in bandages, like white dumbbells. I put them to my head and felt nothing.

"You're wrapped from the neck up," he said. "The nurse on duty at noon peeked through your eye slot and swore you're in there."

He frowned, staring at my eyes. "Yeah, I think I see something ugly inside."

I turned my hands over, burning. It was worse to raise them, so I lay the wrists down on my thighs. I was light-headed, drugged.

"How long have I been here?"

"Oh, all night," Lebowitz said. "Hannah had them put you here by me after they wrapped you up."

I twisted to see down the ward. Everyone in bed looked in worse shape than me. Blood pounded in my ears, behind my eyes, and I began breathing hard, too hard, and tried to stop. I knew I must be shot full of pain-killer, but it burned.

"Where is Hannah?" I asked.

"Resting, I hope. She came down to help when she heard they were bringing you in. After you came out of surgery I made her go away. She'll be on duty in a couple of hours."

I was parched and hurting but I didn't want to lie down again. I wanted to claw the bandages away and try to ease the pain.

"Am I burned bad?" I asked him.

He tried to shrug, as well as he could, stiff in traction with a broken back. He pursed his lips. "I can't see you. But the doc will be around soon. He'll say."

I wanted to ask him if what I'd heard about napalm was true, that it eats into the bones and kills anyway, but I could see his eyes toward the ceiling, his lips tight. He must have dropped a lot of napalm in ten months, so I said nothing.

I put my hand to my mouth but couldn't find a hole. The pain made my thirst worse, and the bandages felt too tight over my nose and mouth. I knew he was watching me.

"How do you get a drink around here?" I asked.

"Nurse!" Lebowitz called. He called again and a girl in blue pants and shirt came to his bed. "A drink for my friend," he said.

I watched her turn and smile. She was about my age. "How you feeling, lieutenant?"

"All right," I said. "I could use some water."

She stayed close. "Sure," she said. "How you doing?"

"It's all right. I'm having a little trouble breathing. It's really hot in here."

I saw her hand reach out to touch my face, but felt nothing.

"There's room to breathe," she said. "It's the anesthesia, but it'll wear off." She smiled. "I'll bring you a shot, now, and some cool water."

She went away and returned with a glass and a plastic tube, which she inserted through a hole into my mouth. I sucked the water and felt it rich in my throat.

"Not too much," she said, and took it away after another sip.

She helped me lie back and raised the gown to give me the shot. She hit a nerve and it stung. She pulled the sheet up to my chest. I had her prop me up in bed with two pillows and she went away again.

Across the aisle was a young soldier with a bandaged chest, a large pink stain on the gauze, his legs spread apart in casts. He stared at my face.

I turned to Lebowitz. "How you feeling?" I asked.

He stared at the ceiling, as if by keeping his eyes straight ahead he might escape whatever he would see with them closed.

"Better," he said. "They say I can travel. The air evac tonight. A C-141 to Japan, then on to the hospital at Scott Air Force Base in Illinois. Two hours from home. I'll be there before Janet even hears I'm coming."

"That's great," I said.

"Yeah."

"Did they find Shackler?"

He shook his head.

"I think I heard him get it," I said.

"That's rotten. How?"

"On the ground, across the river. I heard his .38 and then a lot of firing."

"They say Colonel Dodd is putting him in for the Silver Star."

I didn't say anything.

"Dodd will be around today with a Purple Heart for you," he said. "He likes to do that sort of thing."

I must have slept for hours, and kept hearing a noise with my name on it.

"Mosely? Mosely?"

I opened my eyes and saw the kid with the chest wound across from me, asleep. Then I saw Colonel Tydings smiling at me. I straightened my back and he put his hand up.

"At ease," he said. "I wanted to see how you're feeling. Colonel Dodd wanted to come, but he's flying this afternoon."

He asked me about the mission, about Shackler's chances and when I thought he was shot.

He shifted from one foot to the other. Then he picked up a folder from the bed and showed it to me.

"I've read your first reports," he said.

His eyes looked uncomfortable, impatient to leave. There was nothing more I could do for him.

"I realize they're just your first month," he said, patting the folder, "but they have a different slant. I usually don't get reports this way. But you can work on them back in the States after they fix you up. Send them to me through channels. No hurry. But try to get them done before long. The peace talks are on again in Paris, and it'll all be over soon."

He laid the folder on the bed. "I've made a few comments here and there," he said. "Just to show you how it's done. You talk about some of the men you met and their personal crises over here. All that's true enough, but cut it down. Give us more facts of the good news, something we can learn from after this war's over."

Lebowitz began to cough. I looked at him and he was staring up, his lips clenched.

Colonel Tydings looked at him. "Take for instance that part about Bu Cai," he went on. "You made it sound like the Special Forces camp was a total disaster."

"Bu Cai fell," I said.

"I know that," he said, crossing his arms. "But what we need to know isn't that the camp fell, but that our pilots were flying their asses off to save the ground troops. For instance, take your description of Captain Wayne. Who cares if there was a rainbow contrail or not? What counts is that Captain Wayne and a lot of others were up risking their lives."

He lowered his voice. "How do you think those grunts on the ground felt when they looked up and knew they had the best air support in the world?"

He put his hand on my leg and tapped. "How did you feel yesterday when they rescued you?"

He smiled. "Remember, it's not so much what happens that counts, but how we *feel* about it. That's the value of *SNOW*. Our observations on this war will help us win the next one. There's already been too much bad press."

He glanced at his watch. "I've got to be going, son. And listen. I'm sorry about the Major. He was a good pilot." Then he added, "And so was Captain Wayne."

"Yes, sir," I said.

Tydings walked away and Lebowitz stared at the ceiling. "What the hell," he said.

Later, the nurse came and gave me a few more sips of water, and I had her open the metal clasps of the folder and find the section on Bu Cai. Out in the margin in a tiny precise hand, Tydings had inked-in an addition:

The gallant defenders of the Special Forces camp at Bu Cai, forty kilometers west of Bien Dien Airbase, held out for three incredible days. Although the outpost eventually was abandoned for a strategic move to a more defensible position, once again the dedication of those who fight the air war in Southeast Asia was demonstrated by the professionalism and valor of senior pilots Major Norman D. Shackler and Captain Randall J. Wayne, both later shot down while destroying enemy convoys on the Ho Chi Minh Trail. Major Shackler is still missing in action.

As the Colonel said, good news, something we can learn from. And it was all true.

The nurse gave me a shot and I slept. Later, I looked up and there was Hannah. She saw my eyes and smiled, the corners of her mouth dimpling.

"Hello, Moose," she said, and put her hands on my arms.

"Hannah," I said.

With light behind her, her face was dim but lovely as always, wide eyes and full lips and bare neck. Her cheeks were high and her dark hair lay in loose swirls close to her eyes. She made me think of places far away from Bien Dien, places where we might have met before rockets, before Croom.

She sat near me on the bed and I moved my legs to make room, but she reached out and held them there, touching her. She bent close and peered into the slot in my bandaged face.

"What are you thinking, way inside there?"

"About you," I said. It was burning again, worse than before.

She touched my face. "You're hurting, aren't you? I'll have someone bring a shot."

"No," I said. "Yes. But don't go. Better still, transfer me to your ward."

She squeezed my arm, smiling. "I can't," she said, shaking her head. "They've booked you out on the flight tonight."

"The air evac tonight?" Lebowitz called, his voice high.

"Same as yours," she told him.

"Back to the world," he said, and closed his eyes.

She turned back to me. "I'll miss you," she said.

I shrugged. "Just as well. Croom would kill me."

I saw her eyes blink ever so slightly.

"Where is he, Hannah?" I asked.

She hesitated. "You know Croom," she said.

"I think I do. Where is he?"

"He didn't come back last night," she said, her voice flat.

"That crazy bastard!" Lebowitz said, his face twisted. "When did he go?"

"Late," she said to me, her eyes almost perfect. "After he heard you'd gone down."

She turned to Lebowitz. "I did all I could to keep him." She shook her head intensely at him. "He'll be back," she said. "He'll be back."

We lingered in silence, thinking of Croom. There seemed nothing any of us could say.

Hannah touched the watch on her breast and studied it. She squeezed my arm. "I have to go," she said. She leaned forward, but there was no way to kiss.

"Bye-bye, Moose," she said. "Call me if it ever ends."

She hurried away with her head down. I turned and watched her go down the ward, and before she reached the door her head was up. She never looked back.

Finally, the doctor made his rounds. He looked like an actor I had seen on television and I didn't know whether to believe this was real or not. He told me they had done all they could for me here, but that back in the States I'd be like a new man, with a whole new face. The thing was to get me there as soon as possible. He said I was in for a series of operations and skin grafts, but it would all be worth it.

I wanted to believe him, although I imagined I would never be more than a freak. Back home, he said, plastic surgeons could do wonders with burns. He said they could take skin from where it wouldn't show and graft it on my face and in a few months or years no one would know what happened to me over here. That's nice, I thought. I wouldn't want it to show.

I lay down again after he left and watched the ceiling with Lebowitz, thinking about my face, wondering if I would ever recognize myself again. I tried thinking about Hannah and after the war, but all I could see was an image of her standing against the wall later tonight with rockets falling. I thought about Croom and kept my eyes open on the ceiling so I wouldn't close them and have to picture him killed in the jungle, rotting like garbage, balls sewn in his mouth, his shriveled head staked out in some village and turning black with flies gorging on the crunched semen oozing from his lips.

I kept my eyes open and tried not to think at all. The problem was not remembering. The problem was to let him go.

Later, a tiny flight nurse in blue pants and a pale blue shirt and huge innocent marijuana eyes came and rested her hands on our beds and briefed us on what to expect on the air evacuation. She asked if I wanted to be strapped on a stretcher or to walk on, and I said I'd rather walk.

She and three other nurses finished briefing the others on the ward scheduled for air evac, and soon the corpsmen began transferring the wounded to stretchers and wheeling them outside to the buses. When they came for Lebowitz, I followed and took one of the few seats in the long blue bus, most of it rigged with retaining clamps for the stacks of stretchers. In a few minutes the last from our ward were loaded and they brought aboard the patients from another ward.

At last the sergeant who had helped the corpsmen load got behind the wheel and started the engine, turning carefully away from the ward and onto the asphalt road. The litters creaked as the bus rumbled away. I looked across at Lebowitz on the bottom stretcher and saw his lips tight, his jaw muscles working. I wished for a way to hold him steady to ease the pain.

We rode past headquarters and the barracks and turned down past the track, past the shacks of the Vietnamese. Up high in the bus I could see the fence of the French Club, and once I caught a glimpse of light that could have been a body springing gracefully off the board into the cool water.

We passed the massive sandbagged revetments where F-4s waited, their rocket pods ready. The bodies of four guards loomed above the sandbagged walls, wary. It was almost time for incoming rockets.

How will I live with this, I wondered. Safe on the way to Japan when rockets kill someone tonight. And tomorrow. All the hours of a long year before DEROS. I tried not to think of that, not yet.

We kept going past base ops and on to a road parallel to the east-west runway, turning finally toward the runway itself. The sergeant braked to a halt, the air brakes blasting. After a few minutes the control tower a half-mile away flashed a green light, and the driver churned the bus across the runway and along the west perimeter road, where there were no trees.

I stared as we swayed along, thinking of Croom. The road dipped down and I lost sight of all buildings, and we rode for more than a mile past open fields slanting up on the right and falling away toward the bomb storage dump.

Finally, the road turned sharply to the right and rose over a hill and there on the left was Bien Dien Bay, part of the South China Sea, cutting in north of the base. The sea stretched out, line after line of waves, vast, green, with a strong wind blowing whitecaps all along the shore. I called Lebowitz and pointed and he turned his head to the sea. I was sorry we never got down to the beach. It was beautiful, even if it was mined. I looked out at the waves stretching all the way to Japan and beyond. My face burned again, but outside with the wind whipping green water into whitecaps onto the empty beach, the sea looked cold.

The C-141 waited like a huge white whale on the end of the north-south runway, a thousand yards inland from the sea. Its tail jutted high above the rest of the plane, graceful, like a whale's flukes arched, diving. The low sun gave a thin orange brilliance to the jet. The flight crew waited outside, ready to load. An ambulance truck and two staff cars were there, also, with a squad of air policemen with M-16s spaced in a wide semi-circle around the plane.

The bus wheeled to a stop beyond the back of the big jet, then backed slowly toward the open loading ramp at the rear of the fuselage. They off-loaded us in reverse order, a pair of corpsmen unlocking each stretcher and easing down the bus ramp directly onto the longer ramp of the plane and up into the dark interior.

When all ahead of me had been cleared out, a corpsman motioned and I walked up the grilled ramp into the tunnel of the transport, like entering the belly of a whale. I eased between rows of stretchers locked four high and took a seat facing backward. There were no windows for us, only a tiny porthole deep in the interior. Facing the rear of the plane, I watched them clamp Lebowitz into a middle deck. A flight nurse making the rounds leaned close to him and said something. He answered and she patted his arm and kneeled to the man below him.

Without warning, a boy on a top stretcher in another stack leaned over the side and threw up, the stuff spewing out of him, splattering on the floor and on the ones down below. The boy was as white as his bandages. His head collapsed on the side of the litter and he retched again. Several corpsmen cleaned up the mess without hurry, efficiently, as if it happened all the time. The men down below looked too ill or too drugged to realize what had happened.

The nurse who had briefed me in the hospital came to my row with water and a tube. I sipped it and thanked her. She asked how my face felt and I said it was hurting. In a minute she returned with a needle and sterilized my hip and gave the shot, her eyes wide and faraway.

Unloaded, the bus pulled away and the last corpsmen climbed aboard and began checking their lists on clipboards. In the dusk I could see a lone air policeman, his M-16 slung over his shoulder, his back to the green sea.

I felt a tremor as the first engine began winding up, a deep roar that rose higher and higher and became a shrill whine. One by one the other engines started, and then the ramp began to rise, creaking into place. Then the outer door closed on us like the finish of a giant yawn, as if what we had endured was of no particular consequence. I could imagine what a paltry part I would have in the history books, hardly a footnote to the events of the last few years: Famine in North Africa. Iraq village leveled by earthquake. Last Apollo astronauts walk on the moon. Five-week tour of Vietnam by one Little Moose Mosely.

The door finished closing, paused, then locked and sealed itself. All was dark until dim lights flickered and came on overhead. Air hissed from behind as the interior pressurized. I heard the engines winding up and the heavy jet began to move, rumbling and swaying along faster and faster and I realized with a feeling of doom that we were taking off. I had the feeling of being swallowed, trapped by forces none of us had made alone.

Since all the seats faced to the rear, the takeoff thrust me against the seat belt and I saw the seriously wounded strapped in like corpses, the rigid stretchers vibrating with speed. I wished I could sit facing forward or at least have a window. I wished I did not have to look back.

The seat belt held me while the nose tilted, and in a moment the rumble ceased as we broke ground. I let my arms rest and tried to lean back and let my body sway with the motion of the plane. I closed my eyes to sleep and opened them to keep from dreaming. I felt the shot making me numb and fought it to stay awake.

Soon the pain dulled and the last corpsman sat down and the jet leveled off for the hours to Japan. I tried but couldn't sleep because of pictures crouched behind my eyelids, and finally I leaned my head back and stared at the blank curve of the ceiling, waiting for the pictures to end.